CHANGES IN THE NIGHT

Ruff Justice was lying under the stars, trying to get some rest before the next day of danger, when Wendy Walker came to him. She was naked. Soft and warm and totally female. She lay down beside him, and he rolled close enough to her to feel her quick heartbeat. He bent his lips to her full, firm breast as she lay back, her eyes half closed, her hand on his head, holding him against her.

The first time Ruff had met this woman, she had reached for her gun. The first time Ruff had talked to her, she had made it clear that a mother lode of gold was all she was after. But tonight it was clear that it wasn't gold she wanted most right now. . . .

Wild Westerns by Warren T. Longtree

RUFF JUSTICE #19

FRENCHMAN'S PASS

by
Warren T. Longtree

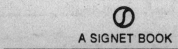

A SIGNET BOOK

NEW AMERICAN LIBRARY

PUBLISHER'S NOTE

This novel is a work of fiction. Names, characters, places, and incidents either are the product of the author's imagination or are used fictitiously, and any resemblance to actual persons, living or dead, events, or locales is entirely coincidental.

NAL BOOKS ARE AVAILABLE AT QUANTITY DISCOUNTS WHEN USED TO PROMOTE PRODUCTS OR SERVICES. FOR INFORMATION PLEASE WRITE TO PREMIUM MARKETING DIVISION, NEW AMERICAN LIBRARY, 1633 BROADWAY, NEW YORK, NEW YORK 10019.

The first chapter of this book appeared in *The Riberboat Queen*, the eighteenth volume of this series.

SIGNET TRADEMARK REG. U.S. PAT. OFF. AND FOREIGN COUNTRIES
REGISTERED TRADEMARK—MARCA REGISTRADA
HECHO EN CHICAGO, U.S.A.

SIGNET, SIGNET CLASSIC, MENTOR, PLUME, MERIDIAN AND NAL BOOKS are published by New American Library, 1633 Broadway, New York, New York 10019

First Printing, April 1985

1 2 3 4 5 6 7 8 9

PRINTED IN THE UNITED STATES OF AMERICA

RUFF JUSTICE

He knew the West better than any man alive—a hostile, savage land rife with both violent outlaws and courageous adventurers. But Ruff Justice had a sixth sense that kept him breathing and saw his enemies dead. A scout for the U.S. Cavalry, he was paid to protect the public, and nobody was faster at sniffing out a killer, a crook, a con man—red or white, at close range or far. Anyone on the wrong side of the law would have to reckon with the menace of Ruff's murderously sharp stag-handled bowie knife, with his Colt pistol, and the Spencer rifle he cradled in his arms.

Ruff Justice, gentleman and frontier philosopher—good men respected him, bad men feared him, and women, good and bad, wanted him with all the wildness of the Old West.

1

IT WAS a simple job, but it bothered Willard Tillits. Find this man called Ruff Justice and put a bullet in his brain.

It was simple because everyone in Bismarck, Dakota Territory, knew the man and could tell you where he was. And Justice had never seen Tillits, never heard of him, so he had no reason to suspect that Willard would want to put a bullet in his brain.

That was on the plus side. The minus was that this Ruff Justice was the damnedest piece of work you ever saw. He spent most of his time squiring a certain lady around—a tall woman with Spanish blood and a body that would make a sculptor weep.

He did that, but this Ruff Justice had funny ideas of what you did with a woman. Willard Tillits had had his own women from time to time. Annie Gates, for instance, who was just fine once you got her off that bum leg . . . But this Ruff Justice was a piece of work. He had caught him, for instance, that one time up in the tree with this Spanish woman, and you had never seen anything like that.

Once, when Willard had been ready to put that .44 slug in his skull and earn the five hundred dollars he would get for putting it there, Justice had gotten up with that woman and started dancing, swirling all around in circles. In the oak grove. In the middle of the night. Naked.

So that was the kind of man this Ruff Justice was. How could you take him serious?

Even down in Missouri Willard Tillits had heard of this Ruffin T. Justice. He was rated pretty high by them that knew. Jack Craig had seen this Justice carve a man up with a bowie knife real bad. They said he was a big Indian fighter. But how could you take him serious?

A man that went walking around with his hair as fine and pretty as a lady's combed down across his shoulders. He was wearing a ruffled shirt the other night and a dark suit with silver buttons—before he shed the whole crop to go naked and dance.

Another night Tillits had seen Justice with a rose in his hair. And this was a growed man who was supposed to be some kind of heller with a gun and a knife!

Tillits hadn't seen a sign of a sidearm, nor of the .56 Spencer repeater they said he toted. Nor was there a bowie knife hanging from him. Maybe there was a weapon up under his coat, in one of those fancy shoulder holsters—Tillits had his suspicions, but he hadn't actually seen it. Anyway, what kind of man wears a shoulder holster.

The voice was coming to Tillits through the trees. He shook his head again, wondering. You just couldn't take the man serious. Not even for five hundred dollars.

"Time weeps with shame at the few glad hours
It's spared for us my dear one
When it knows to love you endlessly
Is all I need for completion . . ."

What it was was poetry. A man out in the woods

with a big-breasted Spanish woman in the middle of the night spouting poetry. Did that make sense?

Tillits listened for a while longer. It didn't get any better. He shook his head as if to shake the poetry out of his ears.

Once some newspaperman back East had found something of Ruff Justice's, something about the Battle of Crossed Lances, about the Indians charging and dying, the sweat and pain of the cavalry as they held them back, and this man—in Philadelphia, it was—had said how Justice was a frontier original, an *American* original, a Westerner, filled with the power of the wild, raw land, and a lot of people had read that poem and they had made him some sort of celebrity so that Justice had toured with the Bill Cody show and read that poem in a lot of places, even in Europe.

The newspaperman must have been drunk.

Tillits crept nearer. He could see him now. See his bare back. He was sitting on a fallen log, looking out across the broad, dark Missouri River. The woman was beside him, her hair down—it was nearly as long as Justice's—her head on his shoulder, her back as bare as his.

Justice had temporarily left off the poetry. His hand was doing something between the woman's thighs. Tillits found that idea very stimulating, but he hadn't come for that. He'd come to put a bullet in the crazy bastard's head and get his five hundred dollars and get out of Bismarck.

"It feels so good," she was saying. "A little higher. Along that little ridge. Oh, God, that's good. Yes."

She held his hand with her own and closed her eyes in ecstasy. They could hear the river flowing past, muttering muted words. Upriver a steamboat whistled although it was nearly ten o'clock. No other sounds drifted to them here in the silent grove. There was only the night and Ruff Justice, and Carmen opened her eyes, turning to him, her lips parting, tugging him down to her, this wild and strong and unpredictable man.

"Do me, Ruffin Justice. Again, please do me. You know the way I like it."

Ruff Justice considered himself a gentleman. Others may have had different opinions, but they didn't know him as intimately as Ruff knew himself. At any rate, he was gentleman enough to do as the lady requested without quibbling.

He rolled her over and down, off the log and onto the soft, dew-moistened grass where Carmen, with heated breath, with her lips parted to reveal her fine white teeth, with her dark eyes shining expectantly, opened her knees to him.

"Let me see," Ruff said, "was this the way you liked it?"

"Any way."

"Or"—he kissed her—"the other?"

"Any, so long as it is quick," Carmen said, and she pulled him down, her mouth crushing itself against his. And it would have been quick, very quick, but for a man from Missouri named Willard Tillits.

Carmen wound Ruff's long dark hair around her fingers and she sighed, staring at him with pleasured eyes. "You are a good one, a good man . . ."

Her eyes opened even wider suddenly and she pushed at Ruff, her fingers clawing at him.

"There, Ruffin!"

Ruff rolled away. With the instincts of a plainsman he moved at the first hint of a threat, diving toward the Colt New Line .41 pistol that sat in its shoulder holster next to his coat.

He had his hand on the Colt when the pistol from

the woods barked. The bullet missed Ruff, spattered Carmen with earth and leaf litter. She screamed in anger and frustration more than in fear.

Ruff, the Colt in his hand, rolled over the log he had been sitting on and dashed for the woods. Another shot followed him, missing his bare heel by inches.

Willard Tillits cursed ... slowly, profusely cursed. He had missed and now he had that crazy man loose in the oaks with a gun in his hand.

The woman, naked and as mad as a wet hen, was sitting on the ground, pounding it with her fists and heels as she ranted away in Spanish. Tillits didn't care about the woman except to notice how she was built.

He started to withdraw, knowing he had a cougar in the oak grove. Justice hadn't seemed like much, but he had moved very quickly. He had known where his gun was at all times, known which way he was going to go if there was trouble ... and now you couldn't hear the bastard.

He was like a big cat or an Indian. Silent.

Unless Justice was lying out there dead or scared, not moving a muscle, then he was as silent as a cougar. Silent as death.

Tillits started to ease away, to move back toward his horse, which was tethered on the other side of the little oxbow. Upriver the steamboat whistle sounded again.

Tillits started on. The arm of a giant oak tree reached across the path toward him and Tillits nearly fired his gun in panic. Looking back, he hurried toward the oxbow.

He didn't know why he was suddenly afraid, but he was. He had discounted the stories about Justice

11

until now. Seeing him strutting around town, you could hardly credit the tales you heard.

It had seemed easy—a bullet in the brain. Five hundred dollars.

Tillits had killed a lot of men and once a woman. All for money. Nothing had ever gone wrong. They didn't know him from Adam, and so it was easy. You just waited and then found them alone or vulnerable. You just sidled up beside them and put a bullet in their brain. And then you were paid.

Tillits tripped over a root and went down in a pile of leaves and sticks. It sounded like a crashing door. He rose again and hurried on. Justice was back there—no matter. There would be another chance, another time, if only Tillits could get out of the oak grove, get to his horse.

And then he saw his horse—across the oxbow, where he had tied it. With relief Tillits started wading the river, wading it as quickly as the hip-high water allowed. The horse watched his approach. Frogs grumbled and croaked in the cattails downstream. The big Missouri flowed past beyond the trees. The stars were huge and silver.

Ruff Justice was there on the shore.

Ruff Justice was there and Tillits felt his heart leap into his throat. He had his pistol in his hand and he lifted it to shoot the naked man. If he could just get a bullet into him, he could take a year off, maybe longer. He could shack up with big Annie Gates and drink whiskey all day and all night.

He jerked his pistol up, but it was too late. He knew already that it was too late. As he tried to squeeze the trigger, he saw the red flower blossom at the muzzle of Justice's Colt, saw the recoil lift Justice's arm, saw the puff of black-powder smoke.

And then, oh God, the mule kicked him square in

the middle of the chest and the fiery spasm of pain erupted inside his chest. He still had the pistol in his hand, but it was useless. It was so damned heavy no one could lift it and fire it. He would never buy a gun that heavy again. They weren't worth a damn. People could just shoot you and you couldn't lift your goddamn gun.

Tillits saw that the smoke was clearing, drifting away in the wind so that the haze in front of the brilliant, close stars was gone. It was gone and then it came back. Blood red and liquid.

"I think . . ." Willard Tillits began, but no one would ever know what he thought. It was incomplete, an impulse the brain had begun to deliver to the uncaring universe before the dark time came and the thought, small and insignificant, was snuffed out by death.

Willard Tillits slumped into the water and, facedown, floated away down the oxbow toward the wide, dark Missouri beyond the big oaks.

On the shore the tall man watched. He was naked, long-haired, and pretty well aggravated. The body of a man he had never even known went floating past and Ruff Justice watched. It wasn't a gratifying sight.

With his gun dangling from his hand he watched until what had been Willard Tillits was around the river bend and out of sight. Then he turned and walked to the man's horse.

It was folded up in the saddlebags. Inside a tobacco tin.

It will be five hunderd if you put a bullit through Ruff Justice. He is apt to be verry much in our way. Know you'll do this as you have always done good work in the past.

13

P.S. Best time with this one is probly when he is sleeping with some woman, which is most of the time it seems.

It wasn't signed. Ruff tossed the note down. He looked to the silent river again and then went back to what he seemed to be doing most of the time. Which was sleeping with some woman.

And Willard Tillits went sailing away toward the Gulf of Mexico a thousand miles away.

2

THE COLONEL didn't look violently angry, nor did he appear exactly pleased. Maybe a little discouraged. He looked at the marshal's brief report and then at the tall, buckskin-clad scout sitting on the wooden chair in the corner of his office.

"Who was the dead man, Ruffin?" Col. MacEnroe asked.

"Couldn't say, sir. He came hunting. He lost."

"*Why* did he come hunting? You must have some idea, Justice," MacEnroe said. The commanding officer of Fort Abraham Lincoln had a habit of tugging at his silver mustache when he was upset. Just now he looked ready to pull it out by the roots.

Justice could only shrug. He really didn't know, couldn't guess. It could have been nothing but someone's drunken notion; it could have been something that ran back a long ways. Ruff Justice, frontiersman, poet, scout, ladies' man, had been down a lot of trails in his time, and he had bumped into a lot of men who didn't care for him.

Some, he suspected, didn't like the way he wore his dark hair, to his shoulders, finely brushed. Or they would take a dislike to the way he talked, walked, the way the women looked at him.

There were some who didn't like Justice because

15

he didn't believe in pushing the small people of this world around and had a tendency to push back rather suddenly for those who couldn't do it themselves. There could be a lot of reasons. This time he didn't have one. The man had come hunting; that was all Ruff knew.

"And the woman—you wouldn't care to tell me who she was?" the colonel asked.

There was a distant gleam in the scout's eyes as he shook his head ever so slightly. "Afraid not."

"All right." The colonel sighed. "I guess that's as far as we're going to get with this." Either Justice didn't know or he wasn't going to tell. It amounted to the same thing. MacEnroe sat looking at his scout awhile longer. Then, with a massive shake of his head he opened the bottom desk drawer, left-hand side, and took out his bottle of bonded bourbon, pouring a dollop into his coffeecup. He didn't offer Justice any. Ruff had never been known to take a drink, for reasons of his own.

"Was that all then, sir?" Justice asked, starting to rise.

"Dammit, no," the colonel snapped. "It's not all. Ruffin, why do I put up with you?"

"Because I do the job," Ruff said with a faint smile.

"No false modesty about you, is there?"

"Never has been," Justice said. "I'm not the best, maybe, but I'm the best the army's going to have for some time, Delaware and Crow scouts included."

"Maybe," the colonel was forced to mutter. He downed his whiskey. "All right, I'll tell you what I have for you. It's the sort of job you're good at, Ruff. Better than anyone I have at my disposal."

Ruff Justice blinked with mild surprise. "If I'd known you were going to compliment me, sir, I wouldn't have wasted time patting myself on the back."

The colonel ignored that. Maybe Justice was in a good mood this morning—MacEnroe wasn't. He rose, walked to the window, and stood with his hands clasped behind his back, looking out at a mounted drill. Sgt. Ray Hardistein's commanding voice was just audible through the log walls of the colonel's office.

"An old friend of mine is out here, Ruff. His name is Martin Spence. Maybe you knew him."

"No, sir."

"He's army. We were with Meade at Gettysburg. A long time back, it seems, doesn't it?" MacEnroe asked, momentarily wistful.

Ruff, who had been there, too—not at Gettysburg, but *there*, in the war, in that time that separated the old generation from the new—nodded.

"Spence stayed in?" the scout asked.

"Oh, yes! Distinguished career. Not too much plains fighting, but he was with Crook for eighteen months over west. Saw some action against the Sioux."

Ruff was starting to get a handle on the man. Now he did recall Spence. Lt. Col. Martin Spence. A big man, as tall as Ruff Justice himself, powerfully built, with black eyes and red, wavy hair.

"Coming back?" MacEnroe asked.

"Yes, I recall him now. What happened to him?"

"Back to regiment and then to Washington. The War College. Then some diplomatic work. Finally liaison to BIA."

"That's right. I remember. He was Washington's contact with Blood Lance, wasn't he?"

"He was." MacEnroe's mood seemed to have darkened. He debated with himself about having another drink, won the debate, and went to his desk drawer. He sat down and sipped this one.

"He's out of the service now?" Ruff asked. MacEnroe was apparently reluctant to discuss any of this, which was odd, considering he had come looking for Ruff. Only later would Ruff understand the colonel's strange manner.

"He's out now. Retired."

"What is it, sir? The job?" Justice had to prod.

"It's a little girl, Ruffin. A little five-year-old girl. The Cheyenne apparently have her . . ."

"No." Ruff said it immediately, firmly. "No, sir. I will not take it on."

"Ruff . . ."

"No, sir. You know as well as I do that there's one chance in a hundred a white child would still be alive."

"We have reason to believe this one is."

"Yes, there's always reason to believe, to hope." Justice stood and stared briefly at the wall, his eyes away from MacEnroe. "You also know," he went on, "what sort of shape rescued women and children are usually in. Why, last year didn't you bring those Woodley sisters in from that Sioux camp? They can't recall their right names, can't speak English except for a dozen words. They'd been abused and scarred and by God they'd lost their souls out there on the plains." Ruff turned and looked at the colonel. His eyes were angry and forlorn at once. "Don't you recall the time, sir?"

"Yes, dammit, I do! I also recall the Spirit Woman business!" MacEnroe was on his feet now, hands flat on his desk, leaning forward toward Justice. "Of course, I realize she was older, a stronger woman . . ."

"I don't care to talk about Louise, sir. You should understand that." Ruff's tight expression underscored

18

his words. The colonel sat down and stared at Justice, saying nothing for a long while. When he did speak again, his voice was soft, even.

"I didn't want to bring her up, either, Ruff. But the point is that people have come back, have been rescued, have survived."

"Not a five-year-old kid."

"They have the best chance and you know it."

"Of surviving *physically*, yes. The least chance of surviving mentally, emotionally."

"If you'd let me tell you . . ."

"I really don't care to hear it, sir," Justice said, and it was as rude as Ruff had ever been to this army officer he worked for. Col. MacEnroe just stared—he hadn't really known how deeply Louise's death had disturbed Justice.

"Justice, damn all—"

The knock at the door interrupted MacEnroe's words. Both men glanced that way. The colonel inclined his head and Ruff Justice rose and went to open the door.

The man who stood in the open doorway was dead. He had one good eye and he stood scrutinizing Ruff Justice with it. There seemed to be intelligence, life in that dark eye, but that was all illusion—he was dead. Grief and fear had burrowed that deeply into his soul. Ruff Justice had seen the walking dead before.

"All right to come in?" the dead man asked.

Ruff stepped aside for him. He had red hair gone to gray, wore an eye patch, and used a cane to walk, a little shuffling walk that slowly, painfully got him across the room to where he lowered his bent frame into the chair Ruff had risen from. He used his hands to lift a dead leg up across the other knee. Then he attempted a smile. It was a very bad attempt, an imitation of a smile like the expression painted on a clown's face.

"Ruff," MacEnroe said, "you recall Martin Spence."

"How do you do, sir," Ruff said.

"Mister Justice." Spence half-rose and stuck out a thin, gnarled hand. "So you're the man who's going to get Marie back for me."

Justice was speechless. He glared at MacEnroe, who couldn't hold his gaze. He murmured something noncommittal and gestured for Ruff to take another chair.

When Justice was settled, he asked, "What happened, sir?"

Martin Spence just shook his head. "I don't know. What happens? Time betrays us." He was silent for a long minute, then he answered more concretely. "You know about the Blood Lance affair, don't you?"

"I know something about it. I know that Blood Lance was ready to bring his band of Cheyenne onto the Pine Ridge Reservation and lay down his weapons if he could get certain firm assurances from the President, Congress, and the BIA. Something went wrong."

"Something went wrong," Spence agreed. "As you know, Blood Lance was—is—a military genius. Not just my opinion, but the opinion of General Crook, who ought to know genius when he sees it. He also had the will to fight. Rosebud was what turned him against us irrevocably. That was a shameful incident—now I can say that.

"After that massacre, Blood Lance and his brother, White Badger, took an oath to fight until the end of time. And they did some fighting." He smiled thinly again, that false smile that looked like a remembered expression the meaning of which had been lost. Ruffin realized suddenly that a part of the strangeness of the smile was caused by partial paralysis of the man's facial muscles. A stroke?

"We tangled a couple of times with White Badger," Ruff said, looking to the colonel. "He's a vicious one. A lot of mutilation, a lot of unnecessary slaughter."

"Blood Lance was never vicious, but then, to the other side maybe the opposing army always seems vicious. At any rate, Blood Lance was good, very good, and he led the army he had at his command brilliantly. What happened, I don't know. They say his new wife, who was part Crow, asked him to lay the war lance down. She said she had a dream of destruction. Some such. You know how the Indians set store by dreams."

"Yes, sir."

"And so he asked about terms. Blood Lance is like Sitting Bull—he's hardly uneducated. Went out of his way to learn English. He reads our newspapers regularly. Well, he wanted things done exactly right. It seems there have been some rumors of Indians being treated unfairly after their surrender . . ." Again that smile was formed, a little more bitter this time.

"He went directly to BIA, I hear?"

"Wrote a letter, or had a captive write it. Which, I don't know, although the hand seemed awfully poor no matter who did it. What Blood Lance wanted was peace. He wanted the right to hunt in the spring off the reservation, the right to own guns for that purpose, the right to govern his own band through the tribal-council system, the right to use Indian police on the reservation."

"And got it?" Ruff asked in disbelief.

"And got it," Spence answered. "In writing. Signed by the Speaker of the House, the BIA, *and* the President of the United States."

21

"Hard to believe. So, what happened? I haven't heard of Blood Lance coming into the reservation."

"And you won't. The treaty's lost."

"It's what?"

"Lost. Moreover, Blood Lance is on the warpath again—changed his mind, it seems."

"Martin," MacEnroe interrupted, "you don't have to go on if you don't care to."

"I know that"—he lifted a hand—"but Mister Justice has come to help me, the least I can do is fill him in."

Ruff and the colonel exchanged another dueling glance. It seemed MacEnroe had been making promises prematurely. Martin Spence cleared his throat, fell briefly into a coughing spell, and began again.

"I was with BIA as the treaty came down, and because of my limited experience out here, I was deemed capable of contacting Blood Lance and handing it to him."

"He wouldn't come in to receive it?"

"Oh, no, not this man! He had read of, or heard of, other leaders being taken prisoner in white forts, at peace conferences. He wasn't going to come in until he had that treaty in hand. But he had agreed to meet with us. I was quite optimistic. Who wouldn't have been? So, with my small party, which included my daughter and son-in-law, their baby daughter—"

"Sir," Ruff interrupted, "I beg your pardon, but why in God's name would you take family along on something like this?"

"Why? Because my daughter spoke the Cheyenne tongue. Studied it for six years, hoping to fill a special need in the BIA. Because my son-in-law was a physician willing to look at Blood Lance's people, some of whom, it was rumored, were suffering from some sort of pox. No, sir, it was not because these

22

people were family that they were invited, but because they were useful, well-qualified components of the peace party." His eye misted briefly and he wiped savagely at it with the back of his hand. "Except for little Marie."

"The girl."

"Five years old. That's all. Five. Bright and alive, laughing . . . five years old."

Ruff looked away, to the window, the patch of blue, cloud-dotted sky beyond. He didn't like this, didn't like it at all.

"Go on," Ruff said, still looking at the window.

"We left Fort Rice on the morning of the twenty-third of March, all very optimistic, pleased with ourselves and our efforts, with the vision of the few members of Congress who managed to push the unique and just treaty through. And then we began to hear the rumors. At Tyler City we heard that Blood Lance had raided a trading post thirty miles west, killing all who resisted. It seemed so unlikely that we discounted it, not being able to find a single firsthand observer of this so-called massacre. Still, it was disturbing. I suggested leaving the girl behind, but my . . . my daughter and her husband were very devoted to her, very. They didn't wish to entrust her to anyone for any length of time—certainly not to a boardinghouse matron in Tyler City, Dakota Territory. Besides, we couldn't really credit the rumors, as I've said. Blood Lance knew we were coming, knew that Washington had given him everything he had asked for—the only time I can recall every single point of an Indian's treaty demands being met. We proceeded. Damn us! We proceeded."

Spence took a minute to get himself organized again. Ruff spent the time glowering at Col. MacEnroe, who had dragged him into this knowing full well

23

that Ruff hated the idea. In his heart Justice knew the little girl was dead, had to be.

How the hell did you tell Spence something like that? He seemed to have very few fine threads holding him to existence, very little to provide him with the will to survive. He had his hope for the missing girl, little else.

"They came down on us, hundreds of them. I saw my daughter . . . She was shot. Mercifully. I was afraid they'd take her alive. The escort and the teamsters—we were delivering some supplies as gifts, items of good faith—all went down in the first few minutes. We were so unprepared . . ."

"Did you see Blood Lance?" Ruff asked.

"No. There wasn't time to look around. But I did see . . ."

"Yes?" Ruff leaned forward intently.

"Never mind. They told me it was because of my wounds. I took an arrow in the skull. Gives you some sort of idea of how hard my head is." Again the twisted smile.

"I'd like to know what you think you saw," Ruff coaxed.

"Whites. There were white men riding with them."

Justice was silent. It made no sense to him. Just now, if there was anything the Cheyenne hated, it was the whites. He couldn't really credit it. Neither was he ready to discount it entirely. He was talking to a professional soldier, and despite the head wound, Spence was probably a more critical observer than most men.

"Go on, Martin," MacEnroe said. "Get to the end."

"Yes." He seemed slightly confused now. "Well, I felt a blow in the back of my skull like a hammer striking me and I went from my horse. I was trampled over—by the wagon team behind me, I think, if it matters. I just managed to see Marie being swept up by someone, a mounted man. One of the Cheyenne."

"Or," Ruff suggested, "you think you saw it."

"I did!" The thin voice grew suddenly strident, challenging anyone to disagree. "I saw that. Then I didn't see anything at all. I went out. I suppose they thought I was dead. Must have. I'm fortunate"—he grinned wryly at his choice of words—"that Blood Lance's people don't go in much for reviling the dead, for mutilation. No one was scalped."

"How'd you get out?"

"Started dragging myself south. Dragging . . . The next morning an army patrol out of Fort Keogh found me."

The colonel interjected, "They searched the battlefield, Ruff. The dead were all accounted for but the girl. It lends credence to Spence's story."

But then the colonel was an old friend of Spence's. And he could afford to believe it. He didn't have to go riding off into Blood Lance's territory to prove it or disprove it.

And MacEnroe, damn him, was sitting there watching Ruff over steepled fingers. He wasn't going to order Ruff to do this. He couldn't. And the broken man, the dead man, sat watching with pathetic hope in his single dark eye. His hand twitched uncontrollably. The big strapping competent officer who would have ridden off himself come hell or high water to find that missing girl was gone, having left this husk in his place.

Damn it all, Ruff Justice thought with savage anger, they're not railroading me into this. He had unfinished business in town with a lady who was just passing through, a lady who liked to dance in the oak grove at night, who liked to climb trees and swim naked in the dark river when the moon polished the surface of the water. They couldn't expect a man to go off chasing ghosts and leave something like that behind.

"As soon as I can get outfitted," he said at last. Then he rose, and with a last scathing glance at the colonel, he went out, slamming the door behind him.

3

RUFF WENT OUT into the orderly room and stood there glaring angrily at the walls. Mack Pierce, the fort's massive first sergeant, was busy with a kid who couldn't have been but thirteen or fourteen at the most. He was standing there in a homemade uniform, holding an old .25-50 Remington in his arms.

"Go on home, Travis," Mack Pierce said with great patience.

"I want to be a soldier," the kid answered.

"And you'd be a good one," Pierce said, "but you just ain't old enough."

Ruff Justice spoke up. "Go on and do yourself some hunting and fishing," he said. "Enjoy being your age. There's plenty of time for fighting when you're older." Too much.

They watched the boy go out the door. "The Grider kid," Mack said. "Comes around from time to time trying to enlist. And I'll tell you what—I'll be glad when he's old enough. He'll shine one day. Now, then, what's for you, Mister Justice?"

"I need some funds, Mack. I have to get some supplies at the sutler's."

"Riding?"

"That's right."

Mack Pierce looked at the colonel's closed door

and nodded, but he didn't say anything else. He just reached into his desk drawer, pulled out a cash box, and passed over some silver money, which Ruff scooped up.

Justice tugged his hat on and stepped out the door. It was bright, cool. The Missouri River flowed past the fort, silver and deep blue. The mounted drill on the parade grounds had ended, but there was still much dust in the air. Ruff looked toward Bismarck, trying to make out the little hotel where she lay waiting. Then, with a swallowed curse he stamped toward the sutler's store.

Damn fools. The world was chock full of damn fools. Spence looking for his granddaughter, knowing she didn't have a chance of having survived. MacEnroe encouraging him. And Justice—well, he supposed he was the biggest fool of all. He was the one riding, looking for something he didn't think could exist. Something to keep an old and broken man alive.

He bought a new canteen in the sutler's store and another blanket, for the nights were getting cool. A whetstone, as his other had wandered off. Fifty rounds of .44s because you never knew. Fifty rounds for the big .56 because sometimes you do.

You expect snakes in snake country. At least you'd better. Ruff Justice was walking right into Cheyenne country, and he expected to find hostile Cheyenne Indians. He meant to travel light and well armed.

The horse was a strapping black gelding named Hadji. He had three white hairs on the tip of his right ear and half a dozen of the same color in his tail. Otherwise, he was as black as obsidian, as sleek and polished. Hard-muscled and deep-chested, Hadji was a lot of horse. He did have his ways, however.

He was fond of reaching back, taking his saddle

blanket in his teeth, and throwing it as Ruff reached for the saddle. He was not averse to nipping at Ruff's legs or arms. Hadji viewed himself as an aristocrat perhaps, above all this foolishness certain horses of the lower classes went through for men.

He was a demon in the stable, but Lord, he was a sweet angel out on the prairie. He floated over the grass, seeming never to tire; he had been born to run, and he knew it. Ruff put up with his other failings. It was always a fair idea to have a big fast animal under you in Indian country.

"Come on, you lazy sack of bones. We've a long way to ride. It'll do you good. Get some of that fat off you."

Hadji's answer was to nip at Ruff's calf. Justice slapped his head away and led him out onto the parade. Col. MacEnroe and Martin Spence were on the plankwalk before the CO's office, and Justice saw Spence detach himself and painfully make his way down the two steps and start toward him, waving a hand. Ruff waited.

"Can't tell you . . . They say you're the best. Appreciate it endlessly." Then he was fishing in his pocket, coming up with a purse. "I'd better give you part of it now . . ."

Ruff frowned. "Part of what, sir?"

Spence stopped, befuddled temporarily. He stood hunched, his cane under one arm as he balanced himself precariously, opening his leather purse.

"Why part of the reward, Mister Justice. Anyone else would have to present Marie to me, but in your case, I'd be happy to advance a part of the sum—"

"A reward?"

"Yes."

Ruff looked across Spence's shoulder to the colonel,

who stood, cigar in his teeth, arms folded, hatless, watching the workings of his post.

"Does the colonel know about the reward?"

"I can't recall mentioning it. No," Spence said.

"You said, 'Anyone else would have to present Marie to me.' Sir—Colonel Spence, have you posted a reward publicly? Do other people know about this?"

Ruff spoke as if to a child. Spence's entire mind was there, but it was a slow-working thing now. That arrow had done a lot of damage. He blinked absently.

"Why, of course. Didn't I tell you that? I've been working my way across the territory, advertising in newspapers, speaking to people, having a batch of notices printed up— My God, man! How else can I go about it? Don't you think I need all the help I can get? I can't do it myself, I just can't."

"No, sir."

"This is the only way I know to go about it. I know that it's a hazardous mission. Hazardous to the extreme. And so I am willing to pay, to pay all I can."

"How much?"

"Pardon me?" He looked at his purse and then to the tall buckskinned man before him.

"What sort of reward did you offer, sir? These posters you've had printed up, the notices in the papers. What sort of reward are you offering?"

"Ten thousand dollars, Mister Justice. Ten thousand gold dollars. All I have or could raise. If I had double, I would give double. Anything to get Marie back." His dark eye had begun to get damp. Ruff turned a quarter away, giving Spence time to knuckle the dampness away.

Ten thousand gold dollars.

In a place and time when a dollar a day was considered a decent wage, when men could labor for five lifetimes and never accumulate that sort of money, it was enough to draw the worst of them all, the scum of the plains. Slowly, silently Ruff Justice cursed.

Spence seemed only vaguely aware of Ruff's verbal excess. He blew his nose and tucked his handkerchief away, reopening his purse. Ruff's hand on his stayed the gesture.

"I don't want your money, Colonel."

"But—"

"I wouldn't take on a job like this for money. I'm not sure I should be taking it on at all . . . not after what you've told me."

"The reward? But, man, I have to get her back! I need men willing to take huge risks. What will they risk their necks for? You know and I know it's gold, only gold."

"You've talked to a lot of men, I take it."

"About Marie, certainly."

"Ever mention my name?" Ruff asked. He had lifted his eyes to the far skies. There were great white clouds drifting in from the north, white, stacked, constantly changing things. Spence took his time answering, perhaps feeling guilt or confusion.

"Yes," he said at last. "I had been in contact with Colonel MacEnroe earlier and he had told me that if anyone could do the job it was Ruff Justice. I had hopes of getting you for the job, of course."

"And you mentioned me to other folks? To others who wanted to help you find your daughter's little girl? For the reward?"

"Yes, I suppose so. I must have."

"All right."

"Did I do something I shouldn't have?"

"No, not at all."

"I simply remarked, if I did mention you, that I had hopes of hiring you on."

31

"It's all right sir, really."

It was all right, except that someone was dead now because he had wanted to stop Ruff Justice. The motive for that still wasn't clear in Ruff's mind, but ten thousand gold dollars went a long way in answering his questions.

He said good-bye to the bent, sad man with the purse and started walking toward the front gate, an anger beginning to simmer in him—an anger at Blood Lance, who had slaughtered the peace party, at those who had betrayed Blood Lance in the first place and shoved him from his lands, at Col. MacEnroe for suggesting him for this impossible task, at himself for being fool enough to accept it.

The anger built and built until he swung up onto the back of the big black gelding and dug his heels into its flanks. Then Hadji leapt into motion, his eyes going wide, his first muscular stride lifting him nearly to a full run. He started fast and he would run long. It suited Justice.

He rode flat out through the gate of Fort Lincoln and out onto the long plains, the wind flattening the grass before him, Hadji's mane and tail stretched out; the long blue skies were dotted with clouds.

He ran the horse for two miles, and by then the anger had burned itself out. He didn't need to worry now about what lay behind him; he had to worry about what lay ahead. The Cheyenne nation, Blood Lance, and possibly, just possibly a small frightened girl.

He turned the horse northward, into the wind, and he settled into the saddle. It was going to be a long ride. Now, with the mad worn off, Ruff could relax and enjoy the day, the black-eyed Susans and lupine that grew everywhere just now. He rode easily, relaxed, but not too relaxed. He still carried his

Spencer repeater across his saddlebows; still his eyes searched the far horizons. It didn't do to relax too deeply in Indian territory.

Besides, there was someone following along behind.

Ruff had seen him a long way back. He was keeping his distance—or they were, it was too far back to tell how many there were. Ruff thought one, possibly a pair, with an outside possibility of another man. There was no dust to gauge by. It didn't matter. One to three men were following him. Following because they had taken off almighty damn fast when Hadji started to run. Now the fact that they were keeping their distance gave them away. Men tended to want company out here, where numbers meant protection, where strangers meant news and needed information about water, Indian movements, roving bandits.

"They're not friends, Hadji," Ruff said, and the ear with the white hairs twitched. Ruff patted the big black's neck and it broke its gait to reach back and try to bite him.

The wind off the north continued to grow colder, the clouds continued to build throughout the day. They were no longer white, harmless constructions but darker and vaguely menacing.

The country was broken hills and sandy coulees. Scraggly cottonwoods and some willow brush grew in the hollows. Here and there an occasional juniper somehow survived. The grass was gray-brown grama grass. Old buffalo wallows pocked the plains, although Justice hadn't seen a living buffalo this near to Bismarck for five years.

The sky began to darken, to take on subtle color. Ruff began to look for a place to camp, although he was wary about stopping—they were still back there. He knew it was three now. He had seen them once clearly against a blue sky background earlier in the day. Three of them—whether they had all started together or not was another matter, but they were all going the same way now. North. Into Cheyenne country. It hadn't always been Cheyenne country. It had been the homeland of the Assiniboins and the Crow, but everyone was moving on the plains. Pushing and shoving, intimidating. The Sioux were drifting toward Canada, some of them, feeling that they would be safer there. Some Cheyenne had followed along.

Blood Lance wasn't looking for peace, no one expected him to go up across the line, but he, too, had drifted.

Justice spent some time wondering what could have caused the turn around in Blood Lance's thinking. He had sued for peace, been granted it, had all his provisions accepted. Then he had turned, violently turned, attacking the peace party under Lt. Col. Spence.

A betrayal? Bad advice from a medicine man? An omen warning Blood Lance? A dream? There was no telling, but Justice would have liked to know. Sometimes such things could be countered. The white authorities had given up on making peace with the Cheyenne warlord. Apparently Blood Lance had given it up himself. That was too bad, for the sake of the people on both sides who wanted peace, who wanted to live life for its simple pleasures, for the sunrise and sunset, for the pleasure of a woman's song. For all the small people like Marie Spence, sacrificed to the war gods.

Ruff camped up a narrow draw. There was no water there, but there were rising bluffs to conceal himself and Hadji. He had his canteen and his tinned beef. He also had his Spencer rifle out and ready.

He no longer saw his pursuers, but he felt them. He *knew*.

And if they had any sense, they would know that Justice wasn't someone you came up on with deadly intent. Not unless you had the will and the numbers.

It had been a long trail and Ruff had put down a few men. Some of them—when he was younger—he had done with a knife, his wrist tied to the other man's in a style of dueling they favored in certain parts of the country. He had killed a few Indians in the line of duty, a few bad men. Some of them he regretted having killed.

That didn't mean he would hesitate about doing it again if it was a matter of their hides or his.

Ruff gave them two hours, then he clambered out of the gulley and stood searching the distances. Their fire was a small one, a mile or so east, distinct against the dark plains. Incautious—but then they were quite a way from Blood Lance's territory yet . . . maybe.

All horse Indians are nomadic, especially in these times of war. Justice wouldn't have been surprised to ride right into Blood Lance. He sort of expected it— that accounted for the hollow feeling in the pit of his stomach.

He climbed back down and curled up to try to sleep. It was cool and in the distance the thunder had begun. He was a long time falling off to sleep, and he wasn't much rested when he rolled out a little before dawn.

Now he chanced his own fire. Against the gray skies, in that draw with the wind blowing like it was, it was doubtful anyone could see it. Besides, he needed coffee.

He had some with dry biscuits, then saddled up after playing a few of Hadji's usual games. He took his time riding out. The wind was at his back, snapping the buckskin fringes on his shirt and trousers. He was riding southward now. Hadji seemed disgusted, or maybe he was a little uncomfortable. It was getting damn cold.

An hour down the trail Ruff began circling back. There was a blue-black wall of cloud across the northern horizon, and Ruff reached back, untying his slicker with one hand. It was going to rain, and rain hard.

He saw no one for mile after mile. Once a scurrying badger turned to challenge him, but Justice had no interest in the powerful, low-built creature.

He found the camp soon afterward.

Swinging down, Ruff walked to it as the first huge drops of rain began to fall, driven against his cheek to sting the flesh and chill it.

There were three sets of bootprints there, marked over one another, but clearly visible. There were three smoothed over patches of grass where the beds had been rolled out.

Justice hunkered down over the ashes, his eye drawn by a small item. He fished it out of the still-warm ashes—a corner of a piece of paper. It was what was left of one of Spence's posters.

. . . years old. Green eyes. Name of . . . Spence.
Ten thousand gold . . .

Ruff looked at it thoughtfully for a time and then dropped it back into the ashes. The rain had started to come down now. Justice swung up on Hadji, figuring he had seen all there was to see. They hadn't left much behind. Just the bit of paper and their bootprints, but that had given Justice enough to ponder. One set of tracks had been small, very very small. Almost like a boy's boots.

Or a woman's.

4

THE RAIN WASHED DOWN and the wind howled. Justice couldn't see much of the time, but he kept Hadji pointed north, into the wind. Lightning crackled around him, now and then far too near for comfort, and it lit up the dark world of the stormbound plains.

Now and then he muttered something bleak and bitter about Col. MacEnroe, who had levered him into this when he could even now have been in the Bismarck Hotel wrapped in a sweet lady's arms watching the rain through a pane of glass with a warm roof over him.

Those thoughts were all he had to warm him. Justice rode through the rain, still turning over the possible identities of his three trackers in his mind. They were up ahead somewhere now, unless they had found a little cubbyhole to stay out of the weather in. It was possible there were many small caves along the river bottom here, but they weren't the best place to be when the water rose.

"A kid or a woman," he said aloud. Either made it appear unlikely that the men he had thought to be following him were gold hunters. Or maybe not. Look at Billy the Kid or Sam Browning, who had killed six men by his sixteenth birthday. Hell, say it was a woman—look at Belle Starr.

Still, they were exceptions. Normally a band of Indian fighters, treasure hunters, a posse was made up of men. Hard men.

Speculation wasn't going to provide any answers. Ruff shook his head as if to empty out his mind. Then he bent his head a little to ward off the rain. He yawned deeply and the rifle boomed close at hand.

He had been crossing a little swale where some water was running, where earlier storms had carried dead trees to be stacked up against some boulders farther on downstream. It was from the boulders that the rifle was fired.

From the corner of his eye Ruff saw the tongue of flame. He heard—or felt—the bullet whip past within inches of his head and he leapt from Hadji's back, sprawling on the earth while a second and a third shot was fired.

Ruff remained where he was. He was covered somewhat by the hollow where he lay. There were six inches or so of cold water in it, but Justice wasn't thinking about comfort just then—he was thinking about staying alive.

His Spencer lay a yard away and he wriggled toward it, sticking out his hand, drawing it to him as three more shots rang out. They all seemed to be from the same rifle, which puzzled Justice. Why not three rifles? Assuming it was the same people, which it damn near had to be. There weren't many reckless enough, crazy enough to be out here in this country

The rain came in with a clap of thunder, the clouds sweeping across the earth, shutting out vision. Justice moved with the clouds. He ran from the swale to the willow brush behind him, weaving through the rain-heavy trees until he was behind the rifleman.

Justice crouched in the willows, the unsheathed Spencer in his hands, his dark hair hanging in his face. He searched the rain-screened land with his blue eyes.

Nothing moved and there was no sound, only the driving hiss of the rain in the willows, the rush of the little stream. Then Justice saw color and he moved. A flash of red in the deadwood and boulders, and Justice was off in a long, loping run, cutting left to avoid a boulder, then right again.

He heard the horse before he reached the deadwood, and he slowed his pace. He walked on in the rain, cursing silently. Ahead, the horseman had vanished into the rain and the clouds. Ruff had no chance of catching up. The black was far back along the creek and the sniper was long gone.

He walked to the trees and the rocks. The rain still fell. The day was all gloom and thunder, matching Ruff's mood.

He found the spot where the sniper had knelt and taken those shots at him, shots that had come near enough to have done the job if Justice had sneezed at the wrong time.

It angered Ruff to have people trying to kill him, people who arbitrarily figured that he should die, that they had a better right to a few more meals, a few more sunsets than Justice did.

There were seven brass casings scattered around the rocks. They were all .44-40s. Outside of that, there was nothing to be learned except that the sniper had been alone.

And that he had worn very small boots.

"Damn all," Justice breathed, looking north. "Damn all if it doesn't look like I got a woman after me."

Which wouldn't be all that remarkable, now that he thought twice. He had met a few here and there.

But he couldn't recall leaving anyone behind that might want to kill him.

He walked back to the black and swung up heavily, first sweeping the rain from the saddle—for all the good that was going to do.

Then he was riding again, wondering.

Justice didn't like riddles; he wasn't good at them. He liked his fighting straight up. Backshooting and treachery were items he wasn't equipped to handle. But that was their game. Whoever they were, that sure as hell was their game.

It was two hours later before he came up on the trading post. He hadn't been past in six months, but it hadn't changed. Donovan's, it was, though the big Irishman was dead and gone, scalped and buried. His partner, Tom Valdez, continued to run the place.

It was built for a fight, and the Indians knew it. There were two palisaded walls, a higher one inside of a lower one, and to scale those was no easy task, not with Tom and his people standing on the higher wall, firing down.

But it had been tried a few times. When Red Cloud was in the area with that big Sioux army, he had bragged he would burn down every white fort and settlement for a hundred miles. He had done it mostly. But Donovan's was still standing. You could see the charred wood on the north wall where they'd tried to burn through and breach it.

Inside, there were four log buildings set in a square, each capable of protecting the others. There were no windows, only gun loops and doors twelve inches thick.

Old Donovan had invited all the local Indians into his trading post when he was through building it. He wanted them to look it over, to understand that he knew what he was doing and he was ready.

Then Donovan had gone out of the fort and they had found him easier pickings.

The Crow still came to trade and sometimes Cheyenne. They had coffee and beans, salt and sugar, hides and furs, corn and trade knives, molasses and blankets at Donovan's. They also had a merry little woman named Carla Valdez, who was Tom's wife and who had come up from dry, treeless New Mexico to Dakota to live with her man. Nobody could make tamales like Carla Valdez.

As Ruff approached through the rain, he saw they also had visitors—three horses standing in the rain before the trading post. There was no one else there but Washta, a Crow Indian.

Ruff passed through the guarded gates, waving to the sentries, and rode to the trading post proper. Washta was there, standing with a blanket around his shoulders beneath the awning, watching the rain fall down, dreaming an old man's dreams.

"Justice," he said in a cracked, deep voice. "Ruffin T. Justice." And then he laughed happily, unself-consciously, with pleasure.

"Hello, Washta."

"Been home, Ruff Justice? Going home to the People."

By the People he meant the Crows. "No," Ruff said. "Not this time."

"A woman, I think she waits still, waits still, Ruff Justice." Washta started to say something else about Four Dove, but Ruff cut him off—there was nothing to say about her, nothing to be done about it.

"Some people just rode in, Washta. Whites."

"Yes, yes. White people. Two men. Then later came a woman, not long ago, Ruff Justice."

"Are they inside?" Ruff inclined his head toward the trading post proper.

"Inside, yes." Washta brightened. "Are you going to kill them all?"

"I hope not. Got a dollar for sweets or whiskey?" he asked. When Washta shook his head no, Ruff handed him a pair of half-dollars. "If you see the People, tell them Ruffin Justice remembers all. He is still their friend."

"And if I see the woman? If I see Four Dove?"

"Tell her Ruffin Justice remembers all," the scout said a little tightly. Then, "Washta, there was a little fight not far north. Blood Lance killed some people who were bringing a peace treaty to him."

"Yes, I remember," the old man said.

Lightning struck across the dark and rolling skies and a split second later thunder sounded to briefly interrupt them.

"You hear a lot. Have you heard anyone say anything about a little girl?"

"Little white girl? No." He grinned. "Not before today, Ruffin. Now everyone asks me."

"There were others here before these three?"

"Oh, yes. Others asking about girl. Yesterday?" He frowned and shrugged. Time wasn't real important to Washta.

"So everyone asks, but no one knows," Ruff said.

"I know. She's dead." Washta put a hand briefly on Ruff's shoulder. "Blood Lance would kill her."

"I think so, too."

"But you look still?"

"I promised a man. Her grandfather."

"So." That Washta understood. "Then you must do it."

"The first three people you talked to—all men?"

"Yes. All men, Ruffin Justice."

"When did they ride out?"

42

"They did not ride out. They are here still. In the trading post."

Thunder boomed again and Ruff looked up at the skies. "I think now I'd better have a look at these people, Washta, at all these people who are so interested in a missing girl."

Ruff Justice said his good-byes to the old Crow and walked to the heavy trading-post door. Putting his palm to the rough weathered wood, he went on through. Tom Valdez himself was just inside, sweeping up. He looked up and grinned broadly.

"Ruff Justice, damn my eyes." He wiped a hand on his white apron and thrust it out.

"Hello, Tom."

Tom Valdez was a tough one. Small, wiry, he had fought Indians, hard weather, and would-be bandits for a long while. Ruff liked him, liked him a lot.

"Carla still cooking for you?" Justice asked.

"Who else can cook like that wife of mine? She's a treasure—even I know it. When a *husband* knows it, well, his wife has to be something."

"I reckon. And I'd fight anyone who disagreed." Ruff smiled. He liked talking to Tom. Valdez was Spanish, but he spoke English with an Irish brogue, having learned the tongue from Donovan. It was a pleasure to see him, a pleasure to be in out of the storm. Ruff took off his slicker and hung it on a wooden peg on the wall.

"You've got some guests here, Tom. Six people, I've been told. All came in yesterday and today."

"It's not shooting business, is it, Ruff?"

"I hope not, Tom."

"I just wanted to move the glass if it was. Hard to come by, you know, and Carla just got a hundred glasses out of Philadelphia—she ordered them three years back."

"And the mirror?"

"The mirror . . ." Tom shook his head. "That's long gone, Ruffin. Black John Torrence came through here about three months ago. He was raisin' hell. Drinkin' trade whiskey and terrifying these little Indian girls I had working for me. He shot one of them—swear, I never would have thought it of Black John. Bullet went right under her arm, creased her breast. Broke the mirror."

"Damn. Never thought he was like that."

"It was the whiskey, Ruff. He started drinking and thinking about his wife—recall her? French girl from up north. Indians killed her. He sat brooding and started his hating of Indians. Ended up taking a shot at this little Assiniboin orphan girl Carla took in."

"Too bad. Where did John drift to after that?"

"Why, if you'd like to visit him, Ruffin, you'll find him out in back there. Not far from the corncrib. You know, where we bury them all."

Ruff nodded. Well, what else could Tom have done? Black John had been a sort of a friend to both of them. An acquaintance, at least, and a good rough-country man. But you can't have people shooting up the help.

"They're all in the dining room," Tom Valdez told Justice. "Five men and a woman."

"The woman just rode in a while ago."

"How'd you know that? Second sight?"

"You could put it that way," Ruff said dryly. "Let me guess also that she carries a Winchester or a Henry rifle—caliber forty-four-forty."

"I see," Tom said thoughtfully. "More than second sight."

"A little more. Tell me, Tom, what would you have done if the one who shot that Assiniboin girl had been a woman?"

44

"I don't get you . . . Oh!" Tom nodded. "I don't know. The way I was raised, the last thing a grown man does is to hurt a woman. But if she'd a shot that girl . . ." Valdez shrugged. "What ain't right for a man ain't right for a woman neither, I guess."

"I guess," Ruff Justice said. He looked toward the dining room. "Have Carla send me in some food, will you, Tom?"

"Don't worry about that. It'll come *pronto* if she knows you're here."

Ruff placed his big Spencer down in the corner beside the coat peg and with a nod to Tom walked through into the dining room.

They were there.

He didn't know any of them. Two big men with red hair—they looked alike, except that the one who was even more vast than the other sat in one corner with a broken-nosed, narrow-eyed man in a town suit. Ruff didn't take to any of them at first sight.

Across the room a man in a blue plaid shirt wearing a bushy black beard sat glowering at Ruff over a half-eaten plate of food. Beside him was a nervous-appearing blond kid with shifty eyes.

It was hard to take to them right off either.

The other one wasn't so hard at all. She was blond and cool and green-eyed and slender, with full, nearly round breasts pushing against the white blouse she wore above a buckskin-colored skirt. The eyes were sharp and quite beautiful. The mouth was sullen and set. Her throat was white and gently curved, firmly muscled.

Ruff Justice walked across the room toward an empty table. Eyes followed him, but no one spoke, no one rose. He sat on a puncheon bench, his back to the wall, his holstered Colt within easy reach. The party with the redheads and the man in the town suit had turned away. The big man with the black beard had gotten back to his noisy and slightly messy eating. The blond kid met Ruff's gaze for a while and then let his eyes shuttle away into the corner.

But the woman kept watching, and Ruff found himself believing that she could pull the trigger on a Winchester rifle like the one she had leaning against the wall behind her.

An Indian girl with a harelip came in, and Ruff crooked a finger at her, wanting to order, but there was no need. Carla Valdez came bustling in, wreathed in smiles, her dark eyes bright and shiny. Justice stood and she hugged him tightly.

"Ruffin, where have you been for so long? Shame on you."

"Army business, you know."

She touched his chin with her forefinger. "Army business—shame on you. I bet you have time for the other ladies, huh?"

"And if you weren't married, Carla . . ."

"Ah, you tease. You always tease, but you're a good man, Ruffin. Mary! Where is that girl?"

"*Sí*, Carla," a dark-eyed, nearly pretty girl appeared with two platters and a pot of coffee. She must have been a half-breed of some kind. Carla treated her like a daughter, scolded and loved her like one as she set the table rapidly, nodding as Carla fired rapid instructions in three languages.

When the girl was gone, she said, "Donovan's girl. She's a good one. But you have to keep them jumping, huh, Ruffin?"

"I think so. I wouldn't know, I never had any kids."

"Well, you eat. Sit and eat. I'll get a room ready."

"No, Carla, I can't stay."

"Why? It's raining. Very cold. You can ride in the

46

dark and rain? I'll let you sleep outside. Everyone else is spending the night, why not you?"

"All of them?" Ruff looked across the room.

"*Sí*. Friends?" she asked softly. "No, I don't think so." Then Carla's eyes lit on the young blonde. "Ruffin, you don't change." She gave him a playful push and went away, admonishing him to eat.

He did, digging into the tamales and corn, the frijoles and fresh tortillas, filling up on warm coffee.

But he didn't taste it much. His eyes, his thoughts, were on something else, on the beautiful blonde who sat staring at him with deep, inexplicable malice in her green eyes. She was staying the night as well, was she? It wouldn't be a bad thought, Ruff decided, to bar his door. She was the one. She had tried to kill him once, and would bear some watching. It was easy-enough work.

But there was no softening of the woman's expression. She hated. She hated, and if she had the chance, it seemed she would try to kill again.

Outside, darkness was falling and the storm ranted on.

5

AFTER SUPPER most of the diners departed for the rooms upstairs in the wooden blockhouse. A couple of them stayed behind. The redheaded men sat there drinking Tom's trade whiskey, glowering at Ruff Justice, growing drunker and meaner.

"You want to maybe see your room, Ruffin?" Tom asked. He wasn't nervous, but perhaps he was still thinking about the glassware. Also, he was worried about Ruff getting hurt.

Justice hesitated. Then he said, "Yes, I suppose so. There's nothing to be gained here. Nothing at all. Do you know who they are, Tom?"

"Yes, I know. Larch brothers. The big one is Dan Larch. The other they call Tiny. He only goes about two-fifty." Tom smiled crookedly. "Heard of them, have you, Ruffin?"

"Afraid so." Tiny Larch had busted up a man in Bismarck, breaking an arm and both legs. He would never walk again. That had been over a spilled glass of whiskey. The law was looking for him but apparently hadn't found him—or the nerve to walk up and try putting irons on him.

Dan Larch was supposed to be worse, harder yet. The stories they told about him were too incredible to be fully believed. They said that he had killed

48

four men at once in a knife fight in Deadwood, that once on a bet he had torn up a quarter of a mile of railroad tracks with his bare hands.

It was farfetched, but when you got a good look at Dan Larch, it didn't seem all that impossible. The meat on his shoulders bulged against his huge shirt. The fists he rested before him on the table were red, cracked, ham-sized. He was huge and ugly and mean-drunk. He was the only man Ruff had ever seen that could make the man next to him come to be called Tiny.

"Come on, Ruffin, I'll show you," Valdez said rather eagerly.

"All right." Justice yawned, stretched, and rose.

It was already too late. Tiny Larch was on his feet. He was balanced there unsteadily, but then Tiny didn't intend to dance. He intended to maul and wrestle and twist and gouge.

"Go on, brother," Dan Larch growled. "Kill the son of a bitch."

"Jesus," Tom Valdez whispered. "Back out, Ruff."

"He'll only come chasing."

"You can't fight the bastard!"

"You mean I can't whip him," Ruff said with a smile. "I can fight him."

"I don't like your hair," Tiny Larch said. He stood near Ruff now, hitching up his loose-fitting home-spun trousers. He blotted out the light behind him, his huge shoulders seeming to fill half the room.

"I don't like your breath," Ruff said with an easy smile. "We're even. Back off now before you get hurt."

"They said you had a smart mouth," Tiny Larch said.

"Who said?" Ruff asked. The question threw Tiny.

He was a lot better at fighting than at thinking, apparently.

"That's none of your goddamn business," Tiny answered after an interval in which the question must have rolled around inside his skull like a stone in an empty barrel.

"All right. Tell you what, Tiny. Why don't we forget all this nonsense? I don't need to have somebody hitting on me. No sense in you maybe getting hurt either."

Tiny's mouth gaped open, maybe out of sheer astonishment. The idea of *him* getting hurt had never entered his small brain. Maybe he never had been hurt.

Maybe he couldn't be.

He was big and powerful and ready, and when he stepped in, his huge right hand arced toward Ruff's jaw. If that one had landed, it might have crushed the side of Justice's face for him, but Ruff had been waiting.

The sucker punchers always throw that one. The big, hard right-hand shot. Finish it off quick and have another drink. It didn't work this time.

Justice blocked it with his left, stepped in instead of backing away, and dug his own right hand into Tiny's wind. He grunted and stepped back, doubled up slightly despite his efforts to pretend it hadn't fazed him. He couldn't even try to pretend about the next one.

Justice whistled a left in past Tiny's guard and it landed solidly on the big man's ear. Blood trickled from it as Tiny staggered to one side, his face going from astonishment to dark anger.

"I'll kill you, scout. Now I will kill you with my bare hands!"

"I hear you talking. Let's see what you've got,"

Ruff taunted. He didn't feel all that confident, but it wasn't a good idea to let Tiny know otherwise. The man had all the edge he needed already; let him think Ruff was fearless.

It didn't work. Tiny came in and started slugging away with both hands, down to the ribs and then up toward the head. Ruff caught the first one with his elbow, but the left landed. The wind was driven from his lungs as Tiny Larch threw a solid right to his midsection.

Ruff covered up and tried to back away. Larch winged a heavy left-handed punch at Justice's head. It rang off Ruff's skull as he only partially blocked it and failed to bob away in time.

That one gave him some trouble. His head was spinning and he could feel his reflexes slow as Larch kicked a chair aside and came on in, still throwing punches with either hand.

A woman, probably Carla Valdez, screamed, and a table went over as Ruff tripped and lurched into it. He still held his fists beside his head, taking Larch's terrible shots as he tried to clear the confusion from his head.

Tiny Larch, confident now, marched in, swinging from the floor, from the ceiling, putting everything he had into each blow. Ruff could hear him grunting through his teeth with each punch.

Ruff had his back to the wall now and he stood braced, weaving from side to side, dodging as many blows as possible, taking those he couldn't dodge.

"Kill him, Tiny!" big Dan Larch shouted.

And what, Justice was wondering, would it have been like if he had drawn the *big* man to fight?

Tiny Larch tried to follow his brother's savage direction. He threw two hard rights at Justice's head. Both missed as Justice went down and then to his left. Still Tiny thought he had his man, was sure he did.

Then Justice exploded off the wall. His head clearing, his eyes angry and hard, his left hand slamming into Larch's face two times, three times. Blood spurted from the big man's nose and he stepped back, blinking. Then, with a bellow he came in again, deciding to answer Ruff's lucky punches with more punishment.

Instead, he met the singing right hook that Justice brought up and over his slack guard. It twisted Larch's head around and sent him stumbling backward.

Larch tried to regain his balance by putting his hand on the round table behind him. Ruff hit him again, hit him solidly, all the good leverage of hip and back, shoulder and arm going into it, and down went Larch. The platter of tamale husks and cold frijoles and half-empty pot of coffee went with him. He sat down on the packed earth floor of the trading post and shook his head, staring dully at Justice.

"I'll kill . . ." Tiny started to get to his feet, but slumped back into the garbage. He tried again and made it. Justice backed up, letting Larch get set. Ruff glanced past Tiny at his brother, who sat there sullenly, one hand on his lap. It didn't take much imagination to realize what Dan Larch was holding under that table, but that would have to be dealt with later.

Just now Ruff Justice wasn't through with Tiny Larch. The big man had enough guts to get up, and he was enraged enough to try attacking Ruff again.

His rage wasn't sufficient. He moved in heavily, his feet shuffling, breathing through his mouth. He swung, and Ruff stung him with a left that caused Tiny to step back again, caused his arms to hang limply at his side.

"Enough," Ruff Justice said. "Forget it."

"The hell with you," Tiny said. He was an insistent man. He swung again, missed again, and Justice put him down. A sizzling right clipped Tiny Larch below the ear and he sat down hard, his arms stretched out behind him. This time when he tried to get up, the arms went and he just flopped over on his side.

Justice had drawn his Colt as Larch went down and now he threw himself to one side. The gun in Dan Larch's hand exploded, the bullet going through the table, crashing into the wall behind Ruff Justice.

Hitting the floor, rolling, Justice fired at Dan Larch. It seemed to be a miss, but Larch dropped his gun, threw up his arms, and slid to the floor, bleeding badly from the chest.

Ruff glanced toward the doorway then and saw Tom Valdez there, his rifle still smoking.

"Thanks, Tom."

"Scum. Serve them right to sleep out tonight. You all right, Ruffin?"

"Right now, yes." Tomorrow he knew what he would feel like. A beating like that leaves a man stiff and bruised, ready to lie down and die.

Holstering his Colt, he walked to where Dan Larch lay. Kicking Larch's pistol aside, Ruff got down and ripped open the big man's shirt. Taking his skinning knife from his boot, Ruff cut away the rancid undershirt Dan wore and looked at the wound.

Dan Larch watched him with sullen, red-rimmed eyes.

"Didn't do the job right, did I?" Tom asked.

"He'll live."

"That's what I meant. Patch him up?" Tom asked Ruff, "Or . . ." He looked toward the back door, toward the little graveyard.

"Patch him up. Don't know why, but go on and patch him up."

Tom turned and nodded to Carla, who had been standing by with bandages and a pan of water, needle and thread. Now she came, and with little clicks of her tongue she examined the bullet wound. The slug had passed through Dan Larch's heavily muscled chest from side to side, cutting a narrow, neat bluish groove from which much blood was flowing. But Carla knew wounds. She used carbolic to clean it, cornmeal to stop the bleeding, then she stitched the man up with needle and thread.

Ruff had to hand it to Dan Larch—he didn't grimace or cry out or curse or turn red. There were only the drops of sweat standing out all across his forehead to indicate the strain he was under, to reveal the fact that he was actually made out of flesh and nerve endings.

Carla was bandaging the man up tightly. Ruff and Tom still stood watching. Tiny had come around, but he was just sitting on the floor, looking at nothing.

"You get out of here, Larch," Tom told Dan.

"I'm hurt."

"You wasn't hurt when you came in here. If you don't leave, you'll be more than hurt, I promise you. I got some boys outside on that gate who know how to use a knife. Get me?"

"Bastard," Dan breathed, and Tom Valdez kicked him in the arm.

"I'm giving you your life. My old lady's patching you together. I gave you food and a fire and a dry place to sleep. You pull a gun and I have to shoot you. Okay. But don't call me unsavory names, Larch. I don't care for it."

"You'll be outside this fort one day. I'll meet you again."

Tom Valdez said, "I hope you do. I never give a man a second chance. By then I figure he ain't gonna learn anyway. Get your brother and get out of here. I'll have your horses brought around."

Carla looked up from her work. "You going to kick him again, Tom, or what? Makes it hard to work. Also if you're just going to kill him, let me know. I got other things to do."

"I'm not going to touch him again. Where's Mary? Mary! Get Willy to bring their horses around. Tell the boys to make sure they get off this post. And I hope to God," he muttered, "that it snows tonight."

It took a while to get them out and throw their gear after them, but then they were gone in the rain, cursing and swearing vengeance.

Ruff and Tom stood on the porch beneath the awning, watching them ride until the gates swung shut and were barred. "That might mean trouble for you, Tom. They said they'll be back."

"Hell, all the troublemakers say that. Look at the place I got, the men around me. Who's going to come back after Tom Valdez? The man that killed me would never get off this post alive, and they know it. So they talk. That's all, just talk."

"I hope so."

"Sure. You're a different story, Ruff. They'll be layin' for you out there. You know that."

Ruff shrugged. "It's happened before. Like you, I don't let the threats bother me."

"Let's go in, Ruff. Have something warm to drink. You'd better let Carla look you over too. A little liniment in the right places."

"No, thanks, Tom." He watched as Tom closed and bolted the massive door behind them.

"I guess this'll send that other dude scurrying back to Bismarck," Tom said.

"What other dude?"

"You saw him—narrow eyes, broken nose. Wearing a town suit. He rode in with the Larches. His name was Canning, Channing ... something like that."

"The Larch brothers were his escort, were they?"

"Something like that. Come on. One more cup of coffee." Tom put a hand on Ruff's shoulder and they walked across the dining room, which had already been cleaned up. Tom got coffee from Mary, smiled at her, and poured himself and Ruff a cup. "Donovan's daughter, did you know that?"

"I heard."

"Yeah, him and his Assiniboin woman. Nice kid."

"Tell me about the dude."

"Channing ... or something. I don't know anything about him. I asked him if he knew what he was doing riding up here, with Blood Lance and White Badger on the prowl, and he more or less told me to mind my own business. The Larch boys, he seemed to think, could handle anything and everything." Tom frowned.

"What did he tell you he was up here for, this dude?" Ruff sipped at his coffee. It was very hot, very strong, with some chickory added.

"He didn't. Well, he gave me some story." Tom shrugged. "Said he was prospecting. I seen his outfit, don't tell me he was prospecting!"

"That's what he said, huh?"

"Sure," Tom replied. "I recall that. Said, 'I'm here looking for gold, just looking for a little gold.' "

Ruff Justice sat frowning for a long while, looking at nothing until Tom asked him what the trouble was. "Nothing, Tom. Nothing at all." Then he finished his coffee as Tom talked for a little while about Donovan and the old days.

The fire in the great stone fireplace was nearly out when they had finished and Ruff, already a little stiff, rose to go up to his room.

"All cleaned up," Carla told him. She carried a lantern as she guided him up the railless wooden stairs. "All fresh linen, clean blankets."

"Knowing you, Carla, I wouldn't expect anything else," Ruff responded.

"Well, thanks, Ruffin. You got manners anyway, not like some who are sleeping under our roof tonight."

"Like who?" They had stopped in front of a door on the upstairs landing. Carla opened it.

"Like that fancy woman with yellow hair. She don't like this, don't like that. Thinks she sees a rat somewhere. So what if she does? Shoot it, I told her."

"I wouldn't give the lady instructions like that."

"Huh?" Carla, who had folded back the blanket for Ruff, turned uncomprehending eyes on the scout.

"Nothing. Nothing, Carla. Thanks."

Then she went out and Ruff was alone in the darkness. He stood silently for a time listening to the heavy rain on the roof. It was louder upstairs than it had been below. Heavy, monotonous. It was going to be a long, long ride if it didn't let up.

He stripped off his shirt and trousers and slipped, shivering, into the bed. He lay there with his hands behind his head, looking at the ceiling for a long while.

Who had sicked the Larch brothers on him? Who was Channing or Canning—they had never gotten the name straight—and what did he want? Just a man after the reward posted by Lt. Col. Martin Spence? Hell, the odds were so bad of anyone ever finding the girl alive or dead that no one but a fool would attempt it at all.

So why were there so many people looking?

Justice tensed. His hand slipped to his gun belt, which hung on the chair near at hand. His fingers wrapped around the butt of the Colt and brought it to him.

There was someone in the hallway. Justice could hear soft steps, hear the floorboards creak ever so slightly. Then his door opened and she stood there.

A lovely blond woman with her hair down, her dress half-unbuttoned, a big Winchester rifle in her hands. Ruff heard her mutter something in a whisper, saw her start to bring the rifle to her shoulder.

Then with an audible curse she lowered it, turned away, and walked up the hall, closing the door behind her.

It wasn't all that easy to sleep the rest of the night.

6

JUSTICE was the first one down to breakfast in the morning. He walked to the front door of the trading post and peered out. It was still raining. Dark as sin, though dawn lurked somewhere behind those clouds. Washta was there, and the old Crow Indian nodded.

" 'Morning, Washta."

"Hard weather. Winter comes early, I think."

"I think so, too."

"I have a good winter lodge here. Warm fire, sweets, and sometimes too much whiskey to dream on."

"I know you do."

"Still, sometimes . . ." He looked beyond the post walls, to the rainswept prairie.

"I know," Ruff replied softly. Sometimes it came on you, a need to ride, to be in the far places, alone. To be cold and a little hungry, to live by your wits and weapons. It came, and sometimes you were just a little too old to do it, to hunt the buffalo in the winter snow and fight off a pack of wolves that wants your kill, to outrun or outshoot the enemy when he wants your blood. "And me," Ruff said, "I wouldn't mind spending a time in this lodge of Tom Valdez."

"When you are old," Washta said, and then his face went dark and perhaps a little sorrowful, "but you will not be old, Ruff Justice. It is in your eyes. You pursue your own end and, someday, you will catch it."

They talked a little more, but Ruff's mind stayed on Washta's prediction for a time. It wasn't the first time he had been told such things and he guessed the words were true. He lived as if he were eager to die. It wasn't that exactly, he thought, it was just that the only time you were truly alive was when you were on the very edge of existence. Well . . . maybe that was madness.

Inside, the others had arrived. Ruff sat down at a corner table and watched as the blond kid, the black-bearded man, and the pretty woman who liked to wander the hallways with a rifle in her hand sat to be served.

" 'Morning, Ruffin," Tom Valdez said. He was newly shaven, wearing a white shirt. "Got an appetite?"

"Not much. Lead a horse in here and bring me a knife and fork."

"Stiff?"

"Not as bad as I'd expected." Ruff rubbed his shoulder. "But I've got a few bruises. That big stud can hit."

"Next time I'd skip the preliminaries and shoot him, were I you," Valdez said, and taken all in all it wasn't bad advice.

Ruff was going to answer, but from the corner of his eye he saw the woman rise, slide her chair away angrily, and start toward Ruff's table.

"I'll scoot," Valdez said. "Let me know what happens."

"Sure. Bring some chow, will you, Tom?"

Valdez nodded. He moved away rather quickly.

The woman was coming at a scurry now, her green eyes boring holes through Ruff, who was looking back calmly, liking the way she filled the yellow silk blouse and the divided, dark-colored riding skirt she wore.

"I have to talk to you." She stopped in front of Ruff, her breasts rising and falling as if she had run a mile, her pupils dilated, her nostrils flaring. A little strand of yellow hair fell across her forehead and curled away across her cheek.

Ruff liked that strand of hair. It made him feel like brushing it away.

"I said," she repeated, "I have to talk to you *now*."

"Without your rifle?" he asked dryly. She fumed but couldn't find an answer.

Mary Donovan sat a pot of coffee and a cup in front of Ruff, glanced with a woman's interest at the blonde, and scooted away, her behind swinging as if to prove she, too, was female.

"Well?" the blonde asked, her voice only slightly less sharp.

"I'd be pleased to speak to you."

"You won't be when I'm through," she said, flaring up again. "Now . . ."

"Sit down, won't you?" Ruff asked, pouring himself a cup of coffee.

"You listen to me," she started again.

"Sure." Ruff smiled. "*When* you've sat down. I feel like a kid in school with the schoolmarm scolding me. Sit down and shout like a civilized person."

Again she sputtered a little, groped for a reply, and failed to find one. She finally sat, and Mary, appearing from the little alcove behind Ruff, brought another cup. She filled it with hot coffee as Ruff sat waiting. Suddenly the blonde found herself in a situation she hadn't envisioned. Instead of standing over a man and shouting at him, she was sitting with him drinking coffee.

"Now," she said, "I want—"

"I didn't get your name."

"Pardon me?" she said crisply.

"I didn't get your name. Maybe you don't know who I am either."

"I can't see what difference it could possibly make."

"It's easier to talk to someone if you know who he is," Ruff told her. He refilled his cup.

"For my purposes, it doesn't matter."

"To you," Ruff interrupted. "To me it does. I always like to know who's warning me off. And who tries to shoot me."

She flushed crimson. "I didn't—"

"Sure you did. You tried it and you missed, and last night you thought very hard about trying to finish the job."

"I *never* . . ."

Ruff held up a hand. "You did. And I'm glad you didn't get up enough nerve to try it again last night. I wasn't asleep, you know. I would have hated to do it, but I would have put a bullet through your lovely breast rather than let you shoot me." He paused and smiled. "I still didn't get your name," he said.

"Why, darn you! You just tell me you were ready to kill me, then you go back to the little proprieties."

"That's life. Changeable, isn't it? Well?"

"I don't know if you're stupid or only arrogant. I do know you're insufferable."

"And better off dead."

"Perhaps!"

Ruff smiled again, and that seemed to infuriate her. She had been crimson already; now that flush deepened and darkened still more. Across her shoulder Ruff could see the blond, weak-looking kid start to rise, see the older man with the black beard place a cautioning hand on his shoulder.

"Well?" Ruff said.

"Well *what*?" She was mad enough to break into tears. Ruff thought she looked lovely in that temper. It tended to make her green eyes shine.

"You still haven't told me your name."

"Wendy Warren," the blonde replied as if she could no longer stand it, as if Ruff's relentlessness had broken her down to where she was powerless to avoid answering.

"Ruff Justice."

"I know that," she said peevishly.

"Oh? I thought you were just out to kill any stranger you didn't care for. Maybe you didn't like my mustache or the way I walked. I didn't know it was *personal*."

She started to rise then, but Ruff reached across the table and gripped her wrist. "All right," he said, "no more games. No more jokes. Tell me what it is all about, lady."

The kid had started to rise again, but again the older man held him back. Terse words were exchanged. Ruff couldn't hear them. He slowly let go of the woman's wrist. She had relaxed slightly.

"It's about gold, and you damn well know it," she spat.

"The reward."

"What reward?" she said astonishingly.

"The reward for the girl."

"What girl?" Wendy Warren shook her head. Her color was paling, her eyes softening.

"Look," Justice said, "suppose we start from zero. Why don't you tell me what brought you out here and what it is you want?"

"As if you didn't know!" She was getting herself worked up again.

"All right." Justice tried to calm her with a smile.

"Let's pretend I don't know. It might surprise you the number of things I don't know."

"The gold," she repeated, clenching her fists, bowing her head slightly so that Ruff could see the arrow-straight pink part in her blond hair. She took a slow breath. "My father had found it. Up near Frenchman's Pass. A big strike, the biggest."

"That's deep in Indian country," Ruff commented.

"I know it is." Wendy finally noticed the errant strand of hair and tucked it behind her pink, round ear. "It's the Indians that got my father in the end."

"You're going a little too fast for me," Ruff said. "I get the general outline, but that's all."

"I'm sure you're better acquainted with these incidents than I am," she said rigidly.

"Well, I'm sure you're wrong. Sorry, never heard of your father or his gold or his death."

"Why, you liar!" she said harshly.

"No." Ruff's voice was steady. "I'm not a liar. I don't know what you're talking about. I don't know why you tried to kill me. I don't know anything at all about a gold strike."

Mary, who had been hanging back waiting for an opportunity, came forward with a plate full of grits and potatoes, sliced fried beef, and two eggs—and eggs were plenty rare out on the plains.

"Thanks, Mary."

"Biscuits will be along," she said pertly, wiping her hands on her apron front, giving Wendy Warren another sharp glance before she turned and strode away.

"Go on," Ruff said.

"I don't know what to say, where to begin. Either you're an incredible trickster, or . . ."

"Say it."

"Or I've been wrong about you."

"There is that possibility," Ruff Justice drawled. "I don't know who's been telling you about me. Maybe that'll come up later? For now, start at the start."

"My father," she began, "was Paddy Warren. He was a prospector for thirty years. For twenty-nine of those, he found nothing but enough dust to keep him going, looking for the main chance, the mother lode, the end of the rainbow. In that last year he hooked up with a man named Dallas Shirke and they finally, at last, hit a big vein up in Frenchman's Pass—you don't need to know the exact location."

"Don't care to."

The girl practiced her frown briefly. "Anyway, they hit it big. Father wrote me—I don't know how many times, I actually only received two letters, you know how the mail is out here—he wrote me that this was it, that he had found enough dust to cover Kansas."

"In Frenchman's."

"I know," Wendy said a little defensively, "it's in Indian territory. But Father reasoned that the Black Hills were once in Indian territory as well, and now the claims there are turning out fortunes for those who own them."

"And all that cost was several hundred lives and the violation of three separate treaties, the end of Colonel Custer and the initiation of a great and continuing war."

"But ..." No, there wasn't any answer to that. Frenchman's was in Indian territory, and that was that. They had outlawed Blood Lance and White Badger, so in a way the claim of Warren and Shirke could be justified, but it didn't hold much water.

"Shirke," Ruff said with disgust.

"You know him, I take it. Or at least he knows you."

"I know him. He's a liar, a renegade, a thug."

"He was my father's friend! He's my friend!"

Ruff's smile was very thin. "Now let me guess who told you that Ruffin T. Justice was a bad man out to steal the gold claim."

The flush had returned to her cheeks, the heat to her eyes. "Yes, all right, it was Dallas Shirke! And was he wrong?"

"Dead wrong," Ruffin said. At least Shirke would be dead if Ruff ran into him again. He knew Dallas Shirke, knew him too well. He killed. He had killed an Indian woman in Kearny and never stood trial for it. He had killed a man—a miner, was it?—in Bismarck and been acquitted.

He was filth, was Dallas Shirke, but he was the sort who was able to put on a face that bespoke honesty and charity and honor while he put the screws to you. Shirke was a confidence man, and very brutal, very brutal indeed.

Why he had wanted Justice out of this was another matter. Ruff couldn't even guess. Shirke sure as hell didn't think Justice wanted his gold. They hadn't met but once, and then—minutes after Shirke's acquittal on the Bismarck murder charge—Ruff had only coolly turned away, ignoring the big bald-headed man.

So why the bother of getting this woman worked up to try ambushing Ruff, why bother to convince her Ruff Justice had to die? For all Ruff could care, she could go her own way, chase down her gold mine, grow rich, and retire to Baltimore to pursue a suitable husband, rings on every finger, gold corset stays, and diamond earrings glittering. He hated to think of her lying scalped out there on the prairie, however. Yet, if she wouldn't be stopped, he wasn't going to try . . . Damn all!

"Where did you meet Dallas Shirke?"

"Where?" she echoed. "In Bismarck. I was with my brother—over there, that's him, Jeffrey—and with Grover. Grover Suggs—he's the man with the beard. I'd received word that Father had been killed, and so we came out to claim our share of the mine. Mister Shirke was quite nice about it. He told us where the mine was. It seems that the law requires us to file again, to put down new stakes. He would have come with us, but he had business in Bismarck that would detain him for another month. That would be a little too late for Jeffrey and myself to establish continuity on the claim. After that, we would have to wait for probate, for civil suits . . . Father never had a will. He planned on living forever, as we all do."

"So Shirke stayed behind and sent you out with your brother and Suggs." Ruff looked at the black-bearded man. "And just who is he?"

"Grover? He is a friend of the family," she said very stiffly. "He used to be a close friend of my mother . . . until she died. He just stayed on to take care of Jeffrey and me when we were little."

"I see," Ruff said.

"You don't see," Wendy exploded, although Ruff thought his remark had been completely neutral in tone. "They were only *friends*."

"I really couldn't care less if Suggs was a defrocked priest who ran slaves to Morocco if it wasn't concerned with this," Justice said, and the woman quieted.

"Well, he's just a friend."

"Fine. Dallas Shirke is a little more—or less—than you think he is, however. He's a crook."

"He is a fine man, a gentleman, unlike some I have met in the West," she shot back.

"All right. I won't argue. Ask around." Justice finished eating, which he had been doing in between sentences, and pushed the plate away. "Now, then, tell me this: did Shirke meet a man named Martin Spence in Bismarck?"

"I'm sure I don't know."

"Think, dammit."

"Spence . . ." She waved a helpless hand.

"A crippled-up older man, a patch over one eye. Walks with a cane."

"I think . . . Yes, I did once see him talking to such a man. I can't imagine what they discussed. It wasn't my affair."

No, but it was Ruff's. He knew what Spence and Shirke had discussed—the girl, and the man who was going north to find her, Ruff Justice.

Which did nothing to explain why Shirke would sic the woman on him.

"What did he say about me?" Ruff asked.

"What did he say?" The color was back in her cheeks. "He said that you wanted the mine . . . that you were the man who had made the Indians kill my father!"

Ruff let her quiet a little. "And how," he asked at length, "did I do that?"

"He said you had an Indian wife. That you were a full-fledged member of the tribe. That I could ask anybody. All you had to do was tell them that you wanted the mine and they would kill my father." She had gotten a little breathless and she stumbled through the last few words.

Ruff didn't laugh. He sat shaking his head. "Well, Shirke is a hell of a liar, isn't he?"

"Is he? You mean . . . But he was my father's partner."

"And he didn't mean to take on any more partners. What do you think he intended to happen, sending you out into this country without an armed escort, telling you to try killing me? He hoped that I'd shoot back or the Indians would find you or the hard weather get you."

"But ..." She was having a hard time reversing her previous convictions. Yet there was doubt in her green eyes now. "What *are* you doing here? You're going the same way we are."

"Yes. But I'm not gold-hunting, lady. I'm looking for a lost little girl because there's just the thinnest chance that she might be alive. Enough of a chance that an old man is clinging to the notion like he clings to life."

"You're so noble," she sniffed, retreating a little from her new position.

"Sure. At least I don't send young women off into the wilderness without any concern for what might happen to them."

"Like Dallas Shirke?"

"Exactly."

"Well," Wendy rose. "I don't know that I believe you, Mister Ruffin Justice. But I'm not quite sure I believe everything Dallas Shirke told me either."

"Does that mean you're through shooting at me for the time being?"

"For the time being." She almost forgot herself and smiled. Ruff waited expectantly for the expression to blossom, but she managed to nip it in the bud. "What must be done—"

"Where is he? That one? Are you Ruff Justice?"

It was the man in the town suit, the one with the narrow eyes and the broken nose who had been traveling with the Larch brothers. He was coming across the dining room with a full head of steam up. His eyes were on Justice and they flared and sparked.

"My guides. My men! You ran them off!"

"The Larch boys?"

Wendy Warren had drifted away a little bit, but she was still listening, while pretending to examine a yellow flower Mary had placed in a narrow-necked pottery vase.

"Yes, the Larch brothers. I've just been told they're gone. I got up expecting to travel on ... and they're gone! Do you know what I paid them to see me through to Frenchman's Pass? A hundred gold dollars. A hundred! And now they're gone and I'm stranded in this blessed wilderness. What do I know about Indians or the frontier? I can't even start a fire properly in the wind! And you—you're the one who did it."

"Yes," Ruff said quietly, "I am the one. Just because they tried to kill me. It annoyed me somewhat."

"What am I supposed to do now?"

"Turn around and go back, I expect," Ruff answered.

"Like hell!" The thin man leaned toward Ruff, resting his knuckles on the table that separated them. "I'll not quit and leave that reward money to you. That's why you're going north, isn't it? To look for the lost little girl."

"That's right."

"And so you thought you'd break up my party, send back my guides. Why, damn you, you're a cheat, Ruffin Justice!"

"Take it easy. If you know my name, you know other things about me. I don't stand for that kind of talk."

"By God, you'll stand for it. You've got a gun and a knife and you're probably a hell of a lot tougher than I am, Justice, but I know the truth. I know the truth." He waved a finger in Ruff's face and Justice temporarily considered snapping it off for him. "You cheated me of my chance, but that doesn't mean I'll quit. Not Carroll Chatsworth!" Then he turned and stamped away.

Wendy Warren glanced at Ruff one last time with a look that said, "I knew you were evil," and flounced off.

Ruff said, "Well at least we got his name straight finally."

"Everything all right?" Tom Valdez, who had just come up, asked.

"Yeah."

"I heard a part of that. I thought you were going to boot his butt out the door—or hers," Tom added, nodding toward Wendy.

"No. That wouldn't have accomplished a lot, Tom."

"No, I guess not. So what are you going to do, Ruffin?"

"Why, the obvious, Tom. Ride on. And take the pack of them with me."

7

TOM VALDEZ tilted his head as if his ears were full of water and he hadn't heard right. "I thought," he said, "that you just told me you were taking those greenhorns north with you, into Cheyenne country."

"That's right, I did say that."

"But why, for God's sake?"

"Because they're going anyway. I don't want Chatsworth behind me with a rifle. I don't think he's as helpless as he pretends. He's carrying a big grudge. The others as well. Maybe if I can keep them all alive for a little while, long enough for them to see a real Cheyenne Indian, they'll turn around and come on back. They're all going to die, Tom. If someone doesn't help them, every one of them is dead meat. You know that."

"Yeah, maybe, but they'll likely take you down with them, Ruffin. I don't see why you just don't let them chance it on their own. What the hell do you owe them?"

Carla Valdez had been listening, clearing off the table. Now she spoke. "Why, Tom Valdez, have you been married that long? If you don't know why Mister Justice wants to guide them all north, why, you've just lost your eyesight." And she stood for a minute looking across the room at the little green-eyed blonde with the splendid figure and pouting lips.

Ruff Justice was looking the same way, and he smiled very slowly. Tom muttered something and went off shaking his head. Carla, dishes balanced in one hand, touched Ruff's shoulder and followed, whispering, "Be careful, tall man. This one, I think she is dangerous."

"You're right there," Ruff said when Carla had gone. "Very dangerous." It didn't make her a whit less desirable. Ruff picked up his hat and started toward her table. It was time to meet the rest of her little party.

"No!"

Jeffrey Warren nearly strangled on his own anger and he came to his feet to face Ruff Justice. The pale-eyed blond kid didn't cause Ruff's eyes to even blink.

"I'm damned if I'll take the man who had my father killed along with us."

"I never heard of or saw your father," Ruff said patiently. The kid was trembling. He had a belt gun on, but Ruff was pleased to notice that the flap of the kid's coat was over it. He didn't need any shooting here.

"You're a liar!"

Ruff's lips compressed tightly. His blue eyes must have flashed a message that the kid understood, for he backed up a step and swallowed hard.

"You don't say that to a man out here, Warren."

"I don't—" The kid began, but the bearded man, Grover Suggs, rose and intentionally interrupted, seeing that the kid was working himself into a corner against a hard man.

"Why not invite him along?" Suggs, who had been the Warrens' mother's *friend*, suggested. "That way we'll know where Justice is, what he's doing. He knows the country, we don't."

"He'll guide us right to the Indians."

"Would you, Justice?" Suggs asked. The black-bearded man's eyes twinkled. He was, Ruff knew, three times as dangerous as Jeffrey Warren. Suggs was under control, always measuring, always alert.

"What's in that for me? I get myself scalped too. I don't know Blood Lance or his brother. Never set eyes on them. Shirke took a half-truth and twisted it around to suit his needs. I am close to the Indians, but the Crows, not the Cheyenne. There's an old man outside who knows who I am and what my relationship with the Indians has been, talk to him. Talk to Valdez or anyone else who has no personal interest in this. They'll tell you. Your mistake, and yours, Miss Warren, was in believing the first thing you were told by a very clever man. You ask around. There's a dozen people on this post who know my background."

"What is it, then," Jeffrey Warren asked with a smirk, "if it isn't the mine you want?"

"Why, didn't you hear that Mr. Chatsworth?" Wendy said smugly. "He wants the reward for bringing back a captured white girl."

"Chatsworth doesn't know what he's talking about either," Ruff responded. "He's letting his own fears feed his imagination."

"Everyone has the wrong idea about you, poor man," Wendy said in a way Ruff found abrasive. He liked the woman despite himself, but damn all, she could be insufferable.

"Could be." Ruff was holding himself back. Maybe he was recalling another time when he had let a party of pilgrims go off into the wilderness without a guide, with scarcely a gun among them, to be slaughtered. They hadn't wanted Justice with them either. They hadn't wanted any help, and so, damn them, they didn't get it.

"Listen," this was the reasonable voice of Grover Suggs, "why don't we check around? Justice seems to have a reputation of varying notoriety with almost everyone. Let's see what we can find out on our own. We could use a guide, Wendy."

"Like a hole in the head," Jeffrey Warren murmured, but no one paid attention.

"Do that," Ruff said. "It's like this, Suggs—if you don't know that country, you're dead before you start; if you do know it, you're likely dead anyway, but it lasts just a little longer. Talk to them. If you can't get them to go back, convince them they need some help." He looked across the room at the sulking Carroll Chatsworth. "Him, too."

"We don't even know him, what do we care about him," Jeffrey Warren said, his voice cracking into a high pitch, like an adolescent.

"I don't know," Ruff said. "What in hell do I care about you? We're here together. Let's try taking care of one another a little."

"And you?" Wendy asked. "Who's taking care of you?"

"We'll see." His eyes met hers and she seemed to soften, to become more feminine under his gaze. "We'll see about that, Miss Warren."

The look she returned was hardly chaste, nor was it submissive. It was an angry, curious, half-convinced, half-challenging look. It didn't reveal a lot, but it did reveal interest. Deep interest. Ruff nodded and turned his back deliberately, walking away.

Outside, it was still raining, but the skies, which had been black and brooding, seemed grayer, lighter, and Ruff walked to the stable behind the trading post to find Hadji.

The black horse was in its usual cantankerous mood and fought Ruff as he saddled.

"Damn you—well, you're still better company than half the people I've met here."

He checked his gear and led the black toward the entrance to the stable. Grover Suggs stood there, arms folded, leaning against the doorframe. Behind him rain ran from the eaves in sheets.

"Riding out with or without us?"

"That's it. I can't wait for you folks to decide what it is you're going to do."

"We've decided," Suggs said, turning his head to spit.

"Yeah?"

"We'd appreciate your guiding us along toward Frenchman's."

"You're all agreed on that, are you?"

"We took a vote. Majority won."

"What was the final vote?"

"Two to one."

"Mind telling me who the one against was?"

"Figure it out." Suggs smiled and turned away. "Oh, the bounty hunter . . ."

"Bounty . . . ? Oh, Chatsworth."

"Yeah. What else would you call him? He says he'll go along too. Justice, I don't know if you're a fool or a madman, or if you're working some kind of game on us. I'll tell you this, in case it wasn't clear. I'd of died for these kids' mother. I'll die for them if I have to."

"For free?" Ruff asked. The needle didn't dig in deep enough to bother Suggs. He had a thick-enough skin to take it.

"For free, yeah." Then he smiled and stepped

back out into the rain, leaving Ruff to stand there with Hadji, wondering. Washta showed up seconds later.

He had a poncho on, his hair braided into a single long queue. He led a paint pony of about three years that wore a saddle, and over the saddle there was a blanket of tight weave, virtually waterproof. He had a sack of provisions tied onto the saddlehorn. He grinned.

"Hello, Justice."

"Washta." Ruff nodded at the horse. "Going somewhere in this weather?"

"Sure. Going with you."

"With me? What are you talking about?"

Washta answered, "Talking about riding with you, Ruff Justice."

"Why?"

The old Crow shrugged. "Everyone else is. Everyone who wants your hide. Maybe you'd like one man along who is your friend."

"In this weather? You have a nice warm winter lodge here, remember?"

"Lodge." Washta made a disparaging sound. "For old women, for children. We are warriors, Ruff Justice. We belong out there."

"Blood Lance is out there. He doesn't like the Crow any better than he likes the whites."

"So? Why do I care about this? Shall I show you the scars on my body the Cheyenne lances, the Sioux arrows have cut? It means nothing. What should I do, sit here and wait to sleep my way to death? Or go honorably, fight and die like a warrior, walk the Hanging Road to where my father and all of his fathers live in contentment and honor?"

"I can't argue with you. If you will come, then you are welcome."

The two men shook hands. "But we won't die," Ruff said. "The death you predicted for me is a long way off yet, Washta."

"Is it?" Washta looked into the distances. Then he returned his gaze to Justice. "Yes, you are right. You will live for a long while yet."

"These men, Washta, I don't trust any of them. You'll see them, make your own evaluation. I see the kid as dangerous because he's weak and uncertain, as a young buck is most dangerous because he feels he has much to prove."

"I think you are right. I saw him outside, watching the door to the stable when I came up. Then he looked at me and left."

"Is that right? I'll watch him even more carefully. The narrow-eyed man, the tenderfoot Chatsworth, is not what he seems to be, but I don't know what to make of him."

"He is a fox," Washta said. "Cunning. If he had longer teeth, he would be very dangerous."

"Suggs, the man with the black beard, is the best of them. Or perhaps the worst. At any rate, he is a man with the ability to look you in the eye. He is either a father to these younger ones or a clever manipulator. I don't know which."

"All three are dangerous?"

"Yes. I don't think any of them would try to harm us until we reach Frenchman's Pass, though. Maybe the boy—he doesn't think, he acts."

"And the woman?" Washta asked. "Is she dangerous, Ruff Justice?" The Indian swung onto his pony's back and waited for Ruff's answer. It was long in coming.

"She is," he said, "more dangerous than any of them."

Ruff led Hadji to the door and swung into leather

as well. Muffled thunder rumbled distantly. They rode together toward the front of the trading post where the others waited, watching.

"Well?" Carroll Chatsworth asked.

"Get your horses. This party's pulling out inside an hour."

In fact, they were on their way within half an hour. It was as if no one wanted to be left behind. They had provisions from Valdez, fresh horses, water, and limitless miles of empty plains ahead of them.

Ruff Justice and Washta led the way, following the rapidly flowing Carson Creek toward the rolling hills that began to rise off the rain-grayed plains ahead of them.

Behind Ruff came a silent, sullen Jeffrey Warren and then his sister. Grover Suggs brought up the rear, carrying his Winchester across his saddle, ready for trouble. Trouble, however, seemed unlikely to come in this rain. The Indians would be staying out of the weather, staying dry. As long as it held, they would be reasonably safe. They hoped.

But it would stop raining and each mile took them farther into Blood Lance's area. They could not travel unseen. Nor did they have enough weapons to frighten off a war party. Blood Lance would come. There would be trouble.

At midafternoon the skies cleared a little. Brilliant fans of golden sunlight spilled through the gaps in the gray clouds and lit the prairie magically. The little rills they rode across had changed to mercury; the dew on the grass became jeweled, alive with shifting color.

Hadji seemed to perk up as the sun returned. Not so Ruff Justice. The Cheyenne would be stirring soon. Blood Lance would be waking, stretching powerful arms, hunting.

The hills lifted higher around them as afternoon faded into evening. Purple shadows collected in the hollows, in the canyons. Here and there they saw pine now with cottonwood in the bottoms. There were many deer venturing out after the rain.

Ruff began looking for a place to make camp. He found Grover Suggs beside him suddenly. The others had dropped back a good distance.

"How far is it now?" Suggs asked.

"To Frenchman's? Two days, with good weather."

"So far?" Suggs looked northward. "I didn't realize, really. Things are different out here."

"They are."

"Look, Justice, I'm starting to get the feeling we were misreading you. If so, I'm sorry."

"All right. No need to apologize."

"Yes, there is. It's just that I have to watch out for Wendy and Jeff. I owe it to their mother. Finest woman who ever lived."

"I see."

"No, you don't," Suggs said rather sharply. "Their father wasn't much good. Not that Paddy Warren was evil, some kind of thief or killer, but he just didn't have a touch with kids, a touch with women. He stayed gone as much as possible, and with Paddy it was possible most of the time. A woman gets lonely . . . I was there and I never regretted it for a minute. Hell, I'm more of a father to those kids than Paddy ever was. Still, I keep my distance, you understand?"

"Sure."

"There wasn't any money left back East when their mother died. This gold claim is all they've got. They are hoping big for it. I mean to see they get it."

"You know what kind of hope they have of working this claim and surviving?" Ruff asked. "What do they think they're going to do? Walk in, collect a few thousand dollars in gold nuggets, and ride out again? They're going to have to work it, those kids who haven't got a callus between them."

"I've got plenty," Suggs said.

"Yeah. Great. Then all you have to do is winter out up here with the Cheyenne on the prowl. You won't even be able to hunt up meat—Blood Lance might hear the shot. You'll live in a dugout, afraid to start a fire even when it is snowing outside."

"You talk as if you've tried it," Suggs said.

"I tried it once. For a friend."

"Then," Suggs said with a shrug, "you know how it is. I know I'm a fool for trying it, but what else can I do?" He looked back at Jeff Warren and Wendy. "Otherwise, they'd have come alone."

"You talk to them," Ruff said. "You tell them how it's going to be up here. Because if you don't get them turned around, they'll be dead before long." Ruff added, "And *that* is not the way a man looks out for two kids he's supposed to love like a father."

Suggs didn't like that, but Justice didn't care. Someone had to impress the seriousness of things on the Warren kids, and Ruff wasn't the one—they wouldn't be likely to listen to a thing he said. Let Suggs try it . . . if he cared to.

Maybe Suggs was something other than he seemed. Maybe he had a little touch of that gold fever himself.

Darkness was filling the sky with deep purple. Ruff saw the little hollow higher up on the sloping, weather-eroded hill and he started that way. It would do for a night camp.

Across the plains a coyote called. Something that sounded like a coyote, at least, and Ruff took a deep, slow, calming breath. Trouble was close now, very close, and the feeling brought an extra chill to the cool evening.

8

......•——◆——►•......

THERE WAS A NARROW OVERHANG above the small alcove where they rolled out their beds. Beyond the mouth of the alcove the horses grazed in the drizzle, which had begun again at sundown.

Washta stood outside the cave, his blanket around his shoulders, watching the long valley, his eyes, which saw things Ruff would have missed and the others couldn't even have imagined, alert and steady.

Ruff walked up beside him and stood there in the purple silence, watching the drizzle fall in the deep valley, watching the dark cottonwoods sway in the wind, watching the long clouds scud past the distant mountains. Far above, far away, a single, tiny patch of crimson marked the vanished sunset.

Washta finally turned. "No. I do not think so. But my eyes are old, my ears not so good."

"They were out there, earlier."

"The coyote? Yes. That was Cheyenne talk. I think a single scout or a hunter calling to other hunters."

"If it was a scout, the odds are he saw us."

"Yes." Washta smiled. "But it would be a time before they could return."

"They will return."

"Oh, yes! Good horses. A Crow. New weapons. A

long-haired scout. And a white woman with yellow hair. They will return. It is a good raid."

Ruff nodded and turned away without speaking. He and Washta were perhaps the only ones who knew what kind of situation they were getting themselves into. Their only chance had been in somehow passing through undetected, in hoping that Blood Lance had moved out of the area. He hadn't. At least there were some Cheyenne here. Blood Lance's people or White Badger's—it didn't matter.

There were Cheyenne on the plains who were at peace, trying to stay at peace, but the majority of those had followed the Sioux north or voluntarily gone to the big reservation to avoid being accidentally embroiled in this war of Blood Lance's. And those who were left had no reason to send out scouts.

Ruff walked into the alcove and sat down on his bed, watching the sky go dark.

"Well?" Jeff Warren asked. "How about a fire?"

"Why don't you just put a bullet through your brain," Ruff answered in irritation.

"What the hell's that mean?" The kid was standing before Ruff and he had his legs spread wide, his thumbs hooked into his belt. The flaps of his coat were back now, giving him access to his Remington pistol. Ruff could have mollified him—maybe—but he wasn't in the mood for cajoling, for baby-sitting.

"It means," he said in simple words, "that it's a damn-fool notion."

"What's that make me?"

"You figure it," Ruff said. "There's Indians out there and plenty of them . . ."

"And whose word do we have for that?" Jeffrey Warren demanded. "Yours? Yours and that old Indian who's a friend of yours and probably half-senile anyway."

"They're out there," Ruff said, just barely holding back his temper.

"Yeah! I seen 'em all over the place today! Hell, this is just your way of trying to scare us off our claim. You might be fooling Suggs with your line, but you're not fooling me, Justice."

"No," Ruff said slowly, "I guess I'm not fooling you."

"And we're having a fire."

"No." Ruff's tone was now hard, steely, cold. "We're not having a fire."

"Why, damn you, I've got a match, and I guess I can . . ." He started away and Ruff tripped him. Jeff Warren went down hard, his skull ringing off the stone floor of the shallow cave. By the time he could get to his feet, Ruff Justice was on his. They stood facing each other briefly, silently. Blood trickled from the kid's nose. Suddenly he let out a yowl of rage and hurled himself at Justice. Ruff stepped aside and tripped him again.

The kid went down again, this time breaking his fall with his hands.

"Leave him alone!" Wendy Warren shrieked. Ruff ignored her.

The kid turned and stood slowly. There was blood on either palm.

"Forget it now," Justice said. "No sense keeping it up."

"I can't forget it now," the kid said, and he tried to draw on Ruff Justice.

Ruff stepped in, clamped his hand around the kid's wrist, and held it there, locking the Remington into its holster. The kid was a lot stronger than he looked, like a lot of young men with that new muscle on their shoulders and thighs. He nearly got the gun up, and Ruff, not liking it a bit, clubbed him beside the ear with a clenched fist.

The kid staggered back and Ruff yanked the Remington from Jeff Warren's hand, throwing it to the far side of the alcove.

"Leave him alone," Wendy shouted again. This time she started toward her rifle, but Washta was already there, holding it by the barrel. He smiled and shook his head at the frustrated woman; she seemed to want to resolve everything with a gun. The whole family seemed to be a little violence-prone.

With another outraged yowl Jeffrey Warren came in on Ruff, his fists flailing wildly. Ruff recognized inexperience, rage, youth. This was no Tiny Larch coming in to kill in a way he had done many times before, but a kid literally having a tantrum. In other places, with other men, he would have taken a .44 through his chest for his trouble. That was the quickest way to end a confrontation like this, and there were plenty of men around who wouldn't have hesitated. They even called it self-defense at times.

Ruff wasn't built that way. He kicked the kid in the kneecap, and he went down again to sit there holding his knee, glaring up at Ruff, not knowing that if Justice had kicked a little harder, he could have made that knee useless for life—not knowing that there were plenty of plainsmen who would have just shot him for a nuisance, rolled up in their blankets, and gone to sleep.

"I'll kill you for this," Jeff Warren growled through his pain. His eyes were filled with tears.

Ruff didn't bother to answer. Washta did, with a grin. "Grow more teeth first, boy. You fight grizzly, you got to have long teeth."

"Shut up," Jeff Warren muttered.

Washta laughed.

Ruff turned away and in the darkness rolled up in his bed. He wasn't gratified by the little squabble. If there was something they didn't need, it was more trouble, especially between members of the party. He tried to sleep then, but he was still angry and it took a long while to feel even drowsy.

"You can give me my rifle now," Wendy Warren said.

Washta was outside near the horses, still watching, listening. After midnight he would wake Ruff Justice to spell him. The day when he could have stayed awake all night to watch for the Cheyenne was gone. Now the eyes grew weary, and when they grew weary, death was not far behind.

"To shoot at Ruff Justice again?" Washta asked as he turned toward the beautiful yellow-haired woman.

"He needs it."

"A man saves your life, the life of your brother, and for that you would kill him."

"Saves our life? By beating Jeff half to death!"

"He played with the boy. He did not try to hurt him, but only to keep him from being hurt himself."

"He knocked him down twice. Kicked him . . ."

"When he could have done much worse. You do not know Ruff Justice."

"And you do. You're his friend, though how anyone could be friends with that arrogant savage is beyond me."

"I am his friend. But I speak the truth, not as his friend, but as a man who has seen war and knows warriors. Justice is known to many people. Many who are not his friends. You may ask who he is. They will tell you the truth, even his enemies. I promise you Ruff Justice did a favor for your brother."

"And let the rest of us shiver and eat cold food."

"A fire would have been a signal to the enemy, don't you even understand that, woman? The Cheyenne would have seen it from many miles away and they would have come hunting. Your brother would not listen to Justice. Now I see you cannot hear and understand either. There is no use talking to such a woman. Here is your rifle."

She took it and stood looking for a minute at the Indian, dark against the dark skies. Then she turned and walked inside the shallow cave.

She felt confused, tired. The road had been long, and every word she heard seemed to contradict every previous word. The country and its ways were unfamiliar. Her anger had dissipated and she felt only numbing weariness. She lay on her cold blanket, another cold blanket over her, shivering, looking up at the sky beyond the overhang. She tried to sleep but couldn't. For the first time she felt uncertain about the wisdom of this trip. They needed the gold, needed it badly, but bad enough to die?

The first time a touch of fear seized her as a coyote howled distantly and she recalled the conversation she had overheard between Washta and Justice about the "coyotes."

She rolled over in her blanket and with wide eyes stared across the cave feeling all of these new emotions—and mingled with them, an even stranger emotion that seemed to swell in her breasts as she lay there looking across at the sleeping figure of Ruffin Justice.

Ruff rolled out at midnight. Washta had touched his shoulder and he had come instantly awake. He nodded silently, sat up, breathing steam in the cold night, tugged on his boots, and got to his feet.

With his rifle in hand he walked to the cave mouth and asked Washta, "Anything at all?"

"No. Very still."

But then the rain still fell, lightly misting down. Once, as they waited there, the moon broke through a seam in the dark clouds, gilding the land and the quick-running rill below.

"Get some sleep," Ruff told the old Crow. "It is far still to our goal."

"Far?" Washta shook his head. "Not far. Death is always near."

Then he went into the cave, leaving Ruff with a bad taste in his mouth, an undefined anger in his thoughts, a distant cold burden on the fringe of memory. He stood and watched and listened. The hours passed and the rain fell. Finally vermilion threads appeared against the eastern sky and a subdued dawn grayed the world.

The others rose stiffly, silently, and they ate together, cold biscuits, water, and tinned beef. Then they saddled their animals.

Even Hadji wasn't up to his tricks. He took the cold bit reluctantly but without fighting it and allowed Justice to throw the saddle onto his back.

Ruff stood a moment looking northward. The first solitary peak stood against the sky, aloof and rugged. Beyond that the mountains began to rise, though now they were lost in the mists. And somewhere was the pass named for the man whose name was lost in history and was known only as the Frenchman, an early explorer lost to the Indians or to the beasts or the terrain or the weather. Frenchman's Pass, where a man named Paddy Warren had found gold, gold he had agreed to share with the devious and deadly Dallas Shirke; where a man hopeful of peace had seen his family taken by the storm of war; where the man called Blood Lance lived up to his name.

"Ready?" Wendy Warren asked.

Ruff turned toward her. She seemed softer this morning, quieter. She held the reins to her dun pony. The wind drifted her blond hair.

"I think so. I hope so . . . If you won't turn back."

"I can't turn back."

"Not even to live?"

"We *need* the gold, my brother and I. We can't do anything else, don't you see?"

"You can learn."

"It was all my father left us. We never knew him. He was gone always, but somehow I think he always meant to become rich for us, to come back in triumph with gifts in his arms, to scoop us up and tell us he was home to stay, that we were wealthy. Time went by"—she shrugged—"and it didn't happen."

"Now you think it has?" Ruff asked.

"I do, yes. I think we *have* to find that claim and take possession of it, you see? If we are to have any link with our father, to complete his dream."

"He couldn't have dreamed of you dying for this."

"Justice," Wendy asked, ignoring that, "who killed him?"

"The Indians, you told me."

"You don't know?"

"I haven't got an idea in the world," Ruff Justice said honestly.

"No, I don't think you do." Her green eyes searched his face. "What I don't understand, then, is why—why are you guiding us to Frenchman's Pass if you think . . . think we can't make it?"

"It's that," he said, "or leave you on your own, and you haven't got a chance that way, lady. Not a chance in the world."

Nor did she have much this way, Ruff noted silently. It was just too far, the risk too big. It was a wonder Dallas Shirke and Paddy Warren had been able to last long enough up here to find the claim, file on it, begin to work it. It showed a lot of guts on someone's part—or an extraordinary stroke of luck.

"There," Washta said, and Ruff looked toward the hill the Crow indicated.

"What is it?" Wendy asked. No one answered. Ruff continued to stare at the hillside, gray in the shadow of the clouds.

"I don't see him," Ruff said.

"Gone now. I saw him, one man. Cheyenne. Not too old. No paint."

"Ah, the old man's dreamin'," Jeffrey Warren said.

Ruff didn't bother to respond to that. Let the kid enjoy his ignorance for a time.

Ruff decided suddenly. "I'm going to go after him."

"To what?" Suggs said.

"He'll be on his way back to Blood Lance now. There might still be time."

Then he heeled Hadji and the big black took off at a run, veering toward the mist-shrouded hill across the valley. Ruff knew he was probably riding a futile race, but there was a chance—maybe the warrior hadn't thought it necessary to run his horse back to the camp. Maybe . . . maybe.

Ruff dipped down through a brushy hollow and began to climb, working the black gelding up the slope, flagging him with his hand. Hadji was nimble and quick, but this was rough country. The sage and sumac were shoulder-high to a horse. Shelves of rock stuck out everywhere, providing further obstacles.

Hadji slipped, recovered, and crested the hill. Ruff's heart lifted with elation. Below him was a Cheyenne

90

Indian brave riding a paint pony. He was moving at an easy canter along an old game trail, riding west and north. Ruff hand-flagged Hadji again and they started down, Ruff's eyes riveted on the Cheyenne. He hadn't seen them yet, or heard them in the rain. If he just wouldn't for another minute . . . one more . . .

The warrior's head came around. He had heard or seen or felt something, and now his eyes opened wide. His rifle went to his shoulder and he fired. Justice saw the puff of smoke first, then heard the report and nearly simultaneously a bullet ricocheting off a rock below him. Shooting uphill off a moving horse, the Cheyenne wasn't much of a threat.

Ruff dug the heels into Hadji's flanks and saw the Indian choose the better part of valor and whip his paint pony into rapid motion.

Hadji came down the slope in a shower of mud and loose stones, going nearly to his haunches. Then he was on the flats too, and it was an out-and-out race.

There was no way that little paint pony was going to outrace the big black. Hadji gained steadily, flying over the ground, reaching its long stride, and maintaining it while the squat Indian pony labored.

If they didn't ride into a bunch of this warrior's friends, Justice had him. The Indian must have suddenly realized that too, for he halted the horse, wheeled it around, and charged directly at Ruff, his Winchester at the level. He fired and the bullet whipped past Ruff's head. The Cheyenne cocked his rifle and fired again, his horse still charging down on Justice.

He had sixteen shots in that needle gun and he figured he had sixteen chances of killing the long-haired white, none of outrunning him.

Ruff Justice admired the logic. He didn't mean to

let those odds matter. His life and that of everyone in his party depended on taking the Cheyenne out. He halted Hadji abruptly. The big black went to hind legs and then settled. It had been well-trained and it stood as Ruff brought the terrible .56 up, sighted, and fired. That Spencer held seven shots, but if it had been a single-shot rifle, it would have been enough.

The big buffalo gun spat a chunk of lead from its muzzle and the Indian took it in the chest. One moment he was waving his arm, shouting, bringing the Winchester up again, and the next he was flat on his back in the mud, a bullet hole through his heart letting the blood leak out of his body and merge with the cold pool of rainwater beneath him.

Justice looked to the far hills. The guns would call them anyway, possibly. If they were within hearing range, they would come riding, looking to see what was going on. And then they would come to kill the long-haired man and the old Crow, the one with the black beard and the kid.

But not the yellow-haired woman. They would take her and amuse themselves with her. Amuse themselves for a good long time, until there was no more left of Wendy Warren than there was of Martin Spence.

Ruff's mouth tightened. He looked again to the dead Cheyenne and then to the hills where the clouds drifted like smoke. It wasn't over, he thought. It was only beginning.

9

THEY KEPT to the deep valleys, avoiding the skyline. The rain came in flurries, helping to conceal them but making the riding more difficult. The battlesite wasn't far, only a mile or two. Above, the mountains began to reveal themselves against the gray background. The cleft in the twin peaks, Frenchman's Pass, was clearly defined as they swung gradually east.

"I don't see what we're gaining going this way," the wet and ill-tempered Jeff Warren said.

Justice shifted in his saddle to look at the kid. He had to peer at him through the curtain of rain that ran from the brim of his hat. "This is what I came up here for. I want to see the battlefield."

"I wasn't talking to you, Justice. I was asking Grover and Wendy what we're going out of our way for. The claim is farther up toward Frenchman's."

"We're all together now," Wendy Warren said. "Mister Justice's business takes us this way. Then he'll escort us toward the claim." She sounded almost human. Ruff glanced at her with some surprise.

The kid was still querulous. "He'll never find that girl. She's dead. Even Justice thinks that. What are we going over the battlefield for? What if she was alive? She wouldn't be there still, would she? What can we find in all this rain after all this time?"

"That's what I mean to find out," Ruff said.

"And what if you find out she's alive and the Cheyenne have her? What are you going to do then? Nothing, just nothing—because there won't be anything you *can* do."

Well, he was probably right there. Justice didn't answer. He had been asking himself much the same questions since Lincoln. The land began to level now and grow wooded. They moved through huge haunted pines as the rain swirled down on a light wind.

Washta lifted a pointing finger and they all saw it then—a broken wagon wheel, partly burned. A little way on, they found the battlesite.

"Battle" wasn't quite the right word. It had simply been a massacre the way Spence told it, and Ruff didn't think he was lying or had a reason to. It troubled him still. Why had Blood Lance gone back on his word? Had the slow pace of the American lawmakers, the dickering, bickering, wheeling-and-dealing United States Congress made him believe there was going to be no treaty? Had it been a planned betrayal from the start? Neither theory held much water. It would have to remain a mystery.

Now they saw the broken wagons, the rusting castaway goods, the weathered, twisted leather, the skeleton of a horse in harness.

Ruff swung down. Washta was with him and Wendy as they moved among the wreckage. The Cheyenne had sorted through the goods the Spence party had brought with them, taking what they liked, leaving the rest.

A tin box the size of a cigar box caught Ruff's eye. He crouched and opened it. Medical supplies, pox serum. It looked as if the weather had ruined the stuff. Ruff showed it to Wendy.

"How many of his own people died because of this attack?" she wondered aloud.

"If they had the pox among them, a great many."

Washta looked at the medicine and shook his head. There were other medical items scattered around, either ruined or mysterious. A stethoscope had been tied in an angry knot.

Wendy found a human skull, and it got to her. She stood frozen, staring down at it, wondering. It could have been Martin Spence's daughter—Ruff thought it was a woman's skull.

"Yeah," he told her a little harshly, "people really do die out here."

"I know, but . . ."

"Yeah, you didn't have to see it. It was only a story. Like a ghost story to frighten you away. Well, it's not quite like that. Think on it."

Ruff toed the skull and then walked away, his Spencer cradled in his arms. A little farther on, he found the rest of the skeleton, scattered by critters. Some of the bones showed signs of having been gnawed on. It wasn't real pretty.

The wagon lay canted to one side, its charred bed black and blistered. Ruff looked around it, hoping to see nothing, finding nothing. Washta did.

It was beside the wagon, hidden in some tall grass. He held it up by one arm. Ruff looked at the doll and felt disgust rise up in his throat. He shook his head and turned away. Washta muttered a single forlorn word in his own tongue.

"What is it? Oh." Jeffrey Warren was beside Ruff suddenly. He looked around, his nerves showing. He was tense and jittery. "Look, Justice, how long are we going to stay here? What are we gaining?"

"It won't be long."

"I mean, you can't find any tracks or anything, can you?"

"It won't be long," Ruff said more sharply.

The kid recoiled a little. "All right. I don't understand this, but I'll shut up."

And damn near time, Ruff thought. He continued to search the area, to walk in a slow circle, studying the ground inch by inch, finding nothing. Time had erased all the impermanent signs of battle. The marks of the horses' hooves had gone, the footprints. Here and there he found a patina-discolored brass cartridge. Nothing else. No bloodstains or feathers or hastily scrawled messages. Death had been all inclusive.

"There will be nothing, Ruffin Justice," Washta, who had also been looking, said.

"No. But you have to look, don't you?"

"How many dead did you count?"

"Ten."

"One more farther into the trees there, but no small bones, Ruffin. No child's bones."

"No, no child's bones."

But that was only negative evidence. It meant nothing at all. Ruff had started back toward the horses when Carroll Chatsworth grabbed his arm and turned him.

"Why are we here?" the narrow man demanded.

"Let go of my arm," Ruff Justice said, and his voice was utterly cold. Slowly Chatsworth let his hand fall away, although there was something in his eyes, something that rose to Ruff's unspoken challenge.

"Where are you going? There's still plenty of light left," Chatsworth said.

"There's nothing to be found."

"We can circle up farther in the pines there. If we get everyone looking, we might discover something."

"It's a waste of time, Chatsworth."

"The hell it is! I didn't come all this way for nothing. I want to find that girl!"

"So do I," Ruff said, and his voice was still cold, threatening. "But she's not here and there's nothing to be learned here."

"But there must be . . ." Chatsworth's eyes narrowed with sudden suspicion. "I see it now. You found something. What is it? You've found something and you're keeping it to yourself."

"Don't be a damned fool," Justice said. "You took a long chance. You lost. Stay here and look by yourself if you want. You won't find anything more."

"Well, that's that, then, isn't it?" Jeff Warren said a little too brightly. Chatsworth scowled at the rest of them and stalked away toward his horse.

"Afraid so." Ruff's voice was still. That was that. What could he do? Nothing at all. Why, then, was it nagging at him that he should do more, that he was leaving a chance unexplored, not making that last effort? No one expected him to go to Blood Lance's camp and look for the girl. He had done all he could do.

Why, then, did it nag at him?

He was in a surly mood as he swung onto Hadji's back and led the way out of the trees toward Frenchman's Pass, a silent, sulking Chatsworth trailing.

Jeff Warren was suddenly animated, excited. Wendy, still remembering the dead woman, perhaps, was subdued. Grover Suggs had been silent for miles. Washta rode with his own thoughts, his mood unreadable.

They began to climb into the mountains as dusk gathered in the clefts and seams of the hills. The rain had stopped an hour earlier, and there were oranges and reds in the western sky. Behind them they could see for miles across the plains.

"Men coming," Washta said, and Ruff's head jerked around.

"Where?"

"Two miles, three. Along the river."

"Cheyenne?"

"White men."

"White men!" Jeff Warren said explosively. "Are you sure?"

Washta explained patiently. "Silver on saddles. Horses' tails are not tied up. Hats." He pointed at the tiny group of figures so far away that none of the others could make out any of these distinctive points.

"Not cavalry, then," Ruff said.

"No."

Not with silver on their saddles. Not in such a small party. It worried Ruff, and it angered him. There was now a much larger chance that they would be spotted. Where he had kept his people to the trees whenever possible and to the low ground, these men were riding on the flats as if they hadn't a concern in the world.

"They'll be seen. Aren't they afraid of the Indians?" This was Grover Suggs, who had assessed the situation accurately.

"If they're not, they're stupid or crazy."

"Maybe we're just *too* afraid of them," Jeff Warren said inanely. No one bothered to answer that simple remark. It seemed to encourage him. "I mean, we haven't even seen an Indian—except the invisible one Ruff Justice went off chasing."

"Oh, shut up, Jeffrey," Wendy said. The miles had been long ones, the weather cold. The dead rode with her now. She was growing less tolerant of her brother.

They rode higher, the day ending in a splash of

color and sudden deep shadow as they searched for and at last found a campsite.

The little valley was wooded. Above it rose a sheer peak and from below there was only one approach, the trail they had ridden. It was as secure a place as they were likely to find.

"How far to this claim of yours?" Ruff wanted to know.

"It's near a place called—" Wendy began.

"Don't tell him that," Jeff Warren interrupted.

"Then how is he going to help us find it? You're getting tiresome, Jeff. Since Tom Valdez's you've been a nuisance." She turned to Ruff. "High Falls, the letters from Father called it. I had the idea it was halfway up the pass. I always figured we could just look for a waterfall—assuming we got this far."

"That's just what we'll do," Ruff said.

"The claim is supposed to be downstream about a—"

"Wendy!" Jeff was standing, fists clenched.

"Half a mile. There are some big cottonwoods growing there—unusual for this altitude," Father said.

"We'll find the spot. But what, then? You can't seriously plan on working this claim. Not in this country at this time of the year, the way the Indians are kicking up."

"We're planning on it," she said decisively, "and we'll do it."

"I wish I could talk you out of it."

"So you can come back and work it on your own, now that you know where it is," Jeff snapped.

"Ruffin Justice?" It was Washta, and Justice walked to him as the others got busy making a cold camp, unsaddling the horses, opening their tins of food, rolling out their beds.

"What is it, Washta?"

99

"They are still coming."

Ruff peered into the darkness below. Finally he picked them out, riding directly toward Frenchman's Pass. They were the men they had seen earlier. Ruff counted six and on his second count made it eight.

"You think those redheaded men have followed you?" Washta asked.

"The Larches?" Ruff shook his head. It seemed unlikely. Tiny Larch and his injured brother riding this far for vengeance?

"Maybe ask the thin man," Washta said, nodding toward Chatsworth, who had been silent since the battlefield exchange. "These Larch brothers were his men."

Ruff nodded. He would ask, but Chatsworth didn't seem to have reason to bring a private army along with him. His own little dream world seemed to have caved in on him, and although he might have been clinging to a private resentment against Ruff Justice, he must have known that there was nothing Justice could have done to find the girl that he hadn't done.

Maybe. People get obsessed with ideas. If Chatsworth really thought Justice was holding out some vital evidence—like what, Ruff couldn't guess—maybe he was angry enough to make trouble. Justice simply asked him.

"Where did you tell the Larch brothers to meet you?"

"What?" Chatsworth's vacant eyes hardened abruptly as they focused on Ruff.

"Where was the rest of your crew supposed to meet you?" Ruff repeated.

"I don't know what in the hell you're talking about," Chatsworth answered, and damn all if Ruff didn't believe him.

Who were they, then? The way they were riding,

they had something definite in mind. Friends of Jeff Warren? Someone Grover Suggs had met, talked to?

Ruff went back to where Washta watched.

"They are gone now," the Crow said without turning around.

"Night camp?"

"I think so." He shrugged. "It is a hard trail in the darkness."

"Could you make out any more detail?"

"Eight men. White," Washta said.

"Nothing else?"

"They ride hard."

Ruff saw to Hadji. He unsaddled, slipped his bit, rubbed his back with a handful of grass, and picketed him in the trees where the grazing seemed adequate. Then he went up the hill a way and rolled out his own bed.

The rain had stopped. The bluff behind them cut the wind. There was even a moon rising beyond the plains. It was a beautiful night. And Ruff couldn't enjoy a second of it. There was death behind them and death ahead of them, and dammit, he only half-understood things out here. There were people with secrets in Frenchman's Pass, and those secrets only made the surviving more unlikely.

He lay there staring blankly at the sky. He was damned near ready to give up on the night when she came to him from out of the trees.

"May I lie with you awhile?" Wendy Walker said, and Justice lifted his blanket to let her ease in beside him.

10

SHE WAS NAKED. Soft and nude and totally female. Ruff didn't ask her why she was there, why she had come to need him. He just rolled to her, feeling her heartbeat beneath his hand, which rested on her full, firm breast. He bent his lips to her taut nipple and teased it as she lay back, her eyes half-closed, her hand on his head, holding him against her.

Ruff rose and he stepped from his buckskins. She was watching him, fascinated by his maleness, her eyes feasting on him.

It was cool out, but beside her it was warm. Ruff slipped back into his bed to move against her, to throw one leg up across her thighs as his hand ran across her soft abdomen to the tuft of downy hair between her legs.

She slowly spread her thighs and reached up to Ruff, drawing him down so that her lips could run across his throat, jawline, meet his mouth and merge with it.

She was suddenly alive, feline, filled with urgent need, with a lithe strength that she put to good use. Ruff rolled onto his back, smiling softly in the darkness, and Wendy, struggling to get a blanket up across her shoulders, straddled him, kneeling across his thighs, her hands on his hard-muscled chest.

She lifted herself now, slowly, with a series of small sounds issuing from deep in her throat as if it were a great effort. She positioned Ruff and then sank onto him, enveloping him in her warmth, shuddering with pleasure as she did so.

Ruff's hand stretched out and caressed her breasts, his thumbs toying with her nipples. Wendy's hair was loose and it cascaded down across her shoulders, silver and bright in the moonlight. She threw her head back and swayed against him, lightly at first but with a deft, ingenuous sureness, her inner muscles clutching at him, teasing the rising need in his loins.

She began to shudder and with both hands she reached down to touch him where he entered her. Ruff saw her lips part, saw her form a soundless word of joy, and then she collapsed against him. He held her to him as he arched his back and, driving against her, found his own sudden hard climax.

She was silent then in the night and he held her to him, his hand roaming her hips and buttocks, the small of her back, following her spine up to the nape of her sleek neck as she relaxed and then finally fell asleep in his arms as the night grew colder.

When Washta came to wake him, Ruff hadn't yet been asleep. He rolled out and dressed hurriedly; it was too cold to be standing around naked.

"Anything?" he asked Washta as they moved away from the sleeping woman.

"I don't know. I feel there is something prowling, Ruff Justice, but I cannot see it or hear it. It is a wolf or a bear or Cheyenne—perhaps the whites who follow us. Something that means us harm. On this night I would be wary."

"I intend to," Ruff answered. "Sleep now." He briefly touched Washta's shoulder, and the Indian walked away, his step light and silent.

Ruff walked to the rim of the valley and looked down into the darkness. There was no fire below, there were no sounds, yet he felt it too. A prickly feeling advancing up his spine, a knowledge that something was ready to burst into trouble.

Who it was, what it was that brought the trouble, he didn't know.

With sunrise they were up and moving. The grass was frozen and there was ice on the horses' backs. Hadji was unhappy and sharp-tempered.

"Will we reach the mine camp today?" Wendy asked.

"Around noon, I'd say," Ruff answered. Then she gave him one quick, meaningful look, a hint of a smile, and she was gone, leading her horse.

"Any sign of our escort back there?" Grover Suggs asked, meaning the eight men who were following them.

"Not since yesterday. Maybe they're late risers."

"Maybe. Is it us they want, Ruff?"

"I'd assume so. We have to. You don't know anything about it, do you, Suggs?"

"Why, no!" Pure surprise, followed by a touch of anger. The righteous anger of the wrongly accused maybe. Maybe something else. Ruff didn't bother to apologize. It had only been a question.

He swung up onto Hadji's back, waved an arm to Washta, and started out. It wasn't far to High Falls if Ruff recollected correctly. The last time he had been in Frenchman's, that waterfall hadn't had a name—or only the Indian name, which meant much the same as High Falls. It was a narrow, sheer fall that divided itself in two as it fell past a granite outcropping and down through the big pines below. A pretty place.

Too bad they found gold there.

The rain began again and they could do nothing but hunch their shoulders, tug down their hats, and ride on. The peaks towered above them as they made their way deeper into Frenchman's Pass. There were boulders strewn about the floor of the pass, washed down by the rain of the past week. Water ran beneath their horses to a depth of a foot or so.

Now they began to parallel the river, the stream that ran down from the falls. Jeff Warren was very excited, nervous, twisting this way and that in his saddle.

The kid must still have been nurturing the idea that he was finished with matters once he had reached the claim. That, once there, his troubles were over, he was a wealthy man.

He had obviously never done any mining work. All he had ahead was weeks, months of backbreaking labor . . . assuming the Cheyenne let him live for weeks.

"That's it!"

Jeff Warren's shout brought everyone's head up. He was standing in the stirrups, pointing up the pass. The falls were a silver silken sheet falling past the rocks and into the trees.

"This is it," he said as if awed by that fact. "This is really it."

Carroll Chatsworth, who had been riding sullenly, silently, suddenly came to life. There was a new light in his eyes, a bright golden-colored light. Wendy had caught the excitement as well. She urged her horse forward.

They crossed and then recrossed the river before reaching the falls. Wendy sat looking up at the waterfall through the pines. The rain was in her face and she looked lovely, fresh, and alert . . . and maybe just a little bit avaricious.

"Half a mile," she said, and they started toward the claim, moving very slowly as if to hold back the moment. "We can't miss it. There'll be signs of work." She looked at Ruff, but her eyes seemed to go beyond him, to some golden dream. He could have been anyone.

That was all right. Justice knew gold fever and he tried not to blame those who got a bad case. Who doesn't want to be wealthy, to live easy instead of sweating, worrying, needing? He had let Hadji drop back, and he and Washta brought up the rear. The two men exchanged an understanding look and Ruff shook his head. The rain misted down through the blue-green pines. They followed the creek around a bend it took to skirt a massive, weather-splintered boulder, and there they were.

"That's it," Jeff said. He leapt from his horse and actually ran toward the mine camp. Wendy Warren, without thinking, followed him. Suggs glanced at Ruff and then walked his horse forward. Chatsworth muttered something indistinct.

The two young people ran to the claim, to the spot where their father had been digging in the river gravel, to where he had washed gold from the sand and sacked it. They went to it and they stood there, eyes gleaming for a time.

Then slowly the light went out as they realized what they were looking at—a place of work. Neither had any idea of how to mine, how to find the fabulous amounts of gold that were supposed to be in front of their noses.

Suggs ambled up to them. He stood looking down into the creek as the rain fell. He crouched down, picked up a rusted pan, and walked to the water, tentatively dipping into the gravel and swirling the pan, gradually bringing color to its edge.

"It's good," he announced. "If it holds up, it's real good."

"Enough to make us rich?" Jeff wanted to know.

"Enough for that. If we can get it out."

"We can, we will. You'll show us what to do, won't you, Grover? Good old Grover. Mother could always count on you. We can too."

"Sure," Grover Suggs said. "You can count on me."

Then a new voice broke into the clearing. "Touching."

Ruff turned very slowly to see the eight men emerge from the trees. All were armed and there was no point at all in trying to fight them, but that message didn't get through to Carroll Chatsworth's brain. In panic he reached for his gun and someone shot him. He was blown back against a tree to slam into it and slide to the ground as the rain fell; he twitched just a little before the life leaked out of his narrow body.

"The rest of you can put your weapons down politely," the leader of the newcomers said. Justice knew him now. It was Dallas Shirke.

Wendy just stared defiantly at the man. "What are you doing here? Why did you kill that man?"

"Just protecting my claim from intruders."

"Your claim?"

"That's right. I thought I told you I had legal claim," Dallas Shirke said, swinging down from his blue roan. He removed his hat and dabbed briefly at his bald head.

"It's my father's claim," Wendy said, nearly shouting.

"That's right, honey," he said at last with mock sympathy. "It was his and mine. He found it and I became a sort of silent partner after an all-night poker game."

"It's as much ours as yours," Jeff Warren said,

striding up to Dallas Shirke. "I'd like to know what in hell is going on."

Dallas showed him. He backhanded him across the face and the kid sat down in the riverside mud. He had an idea of going for his gun, which hadn't been shed yet, but one of Shirke's people lifted it from his holster.

"That's what's going on," Shirke said.

"This is our claim," Jeff repeated.

"Right." Shirke looked around. "The kid's not too smart, is he?"

"What happened to my father?" Wendy Warren asked with sudden knowledge.

"Why, I believe it was the Indians," Shirke said with a nasty little smile.

"You . . ." She leapt at Shirke and he clubbed her down. It was too much for Justice, and he made his move, going at Shirke's throat; but there were too many of them and they knocked Justice down before he could reach the man, knocked him down and kept him down. One man with an eye patch kicked Ruff under his lowest rib on the right side, and pain shot through the scout's body as his liver was jarred.

"You ain't too smart either, Justice, not as smart as I used to think you were. What in hell are you doing involved in this anyway?"

Ruff didn't answer. It would have hurt to speak, but he didn't want Shirke to know that. He simply sat there staring up at the bald man through his long hair.

"You killed him," Wendy said. She had risen. She faced Shirke with mud on her hands, her blousefront, her knees.

Shirke didn't bother answering.

"What's going to happen to them? To us?" Grover Suggs asked.

"Who knows?" Shirke looked around. "There are a lot of things that could happen out here. The Indians, I expect, will get you."

"You rotten bastard," Jeff Warren said.

Shirke didn't answer. He had been called worse things.

"Is that why you sent us out here?" Wendy asked, still unable to believe that anyone could be so calculatingly wicked. "So that you could kill us and everyone would just blame it on the Indians, say what fools we were to come up here?"

"Smart, isn't she? See, Justice, there's one smart one in every group."

Ruff was getting to his feet, holding his side, wondering if he could possibly get to the skinning knife inside his boot and cut Shirke's throat for him before they gunned him down. It was mad, useless, even if he could have accomplished it, but Ruff's brain was lighted coldly with thoughts of vengeance.

"There's really no need to kill us," Jeff Warren said shakily. The kid looked very young now, frightened. Well, he had the right to look frightened. "We could just sign over our share of the mine to you. I'll do it right now! Sure. Have you got a pencil and paper?"

"Shut up, kid."

"Don't you think I'm serious?" Jeff asked pleadingly.

"He knows you are," Grover Suggs said. "He just can't take the chance on you going back and telling what happened out here."

"But if he has the legal claim . . ." Jeff was falling apart. He looked desperately to Suggs and then to Shirke, finally to Ruff Justice, as if the scout somehow held some trump card. He didn't. He could only watch as the rain fell down and Dallas Shirke's men sat their horses, guns in hand, awaiting the order.

"Where do you want to do it?" one of Shirke's men asked, the one-eyed man who had a coldness to him, the coldness of a corpse. Dallas Shirke called him Connolly.

"I don't care. Anywhere."

"Can we have the woman first?"

"Just kill 'em, Connolly. Scalp 'em, I guess. Just in case someone stumbles past."

"Who? Army ain't got the guts to come in here."

"Yeah, we'll discuss it later. For now, do it!" Shirke said, turning on his heel sharply.

Ruff was ready to try it now. It wouldn't gain them anything in the end, but at least Shirke would be dead. He began to crouch, to reach toward his skinning knife. Washta was watching him, his own desperate scheme in his head. Shirke's crew had dismounted and they circled Ruff and the gold party.

They were going to die. It was that simple.

There was no sound but the rain falling, the soughing of the wind in the pines, the whispers of the creek running past. There was no sound at all, no movement.

And then the Indians were there. They might have materialized out of thin air, grown from the earth itself. They weren't there and then they were. A dozen of them, all armed, all afoot. They looked at Shirke and he looked back. Their leader stepped forward.

"You are going to kill them?" the Cheyenne asked in excellent English.

"That's right, Blood Lance."

"Very well. Kill them, then," the Cheyenne war leader replied.

11

BLOOD LANCE was very tall. He wore paint faded by the rain and time. His hair was knotted on one side of his head. Feathers and silver beads were tied into it, as was a length of fox fur. He was shirtless, wearing leggings, loincloth, moccasins. In his hand was a new Henry repeater.

He looked at Ruff and the girl and said, "Kill them, Shirke, but not here. At the camp. Let my people be amused."

"Listen, Blood Lance," Shirke began hotly. "Your brother told me—"

"I do not care what White Badger said. Do what I tell you to do, Shirke. Do it now."

Ruff looked at the two men, trying to understand the connection between them. There was antagonism, but obviously a sort of treaty as well. Shirke was free to come and go to his claim, to do as he wanted. Except that Blood Lance didn't care for Shirke, didn't care for the informal treaty—that much was obvious. Then, why keep it?

There wasn't time to ponder it. They were being herded toward their horses, roughly pushed forward by the Indians. Other Indians emerged from the trees, bringing the Cheyenne horses. Ruff swung aboard Hadji and immediately a loop was thrown around his shoulders. The Cheyenne holding the other end of the leather reata was eyeing Ruff's long hair in a way Justice didn't care for.

"Give me the chance and I'll take *yours*," Ruff said quietly.

The Indian frowned. Perhaps he understood, perhaps not. Then to amuse himself, he made a pass at Ruff's head with a war hatchet. Justice didn't flinch and that bothered the Indian just a little.

"Enough of that foolishness, Cougar Time," Blood Lance said impatiently.

He looked at Ruff and then started on his way. "Thank you," Ruff said in the Cheyenne tongue, and Blood Lance halted to look back at the long-haired scout. "I did not want to endure a child's game all the way to your camp."

"You speak our tongue."

"As a boy might. A few words."

"Later we will talk."

"Talk? Do you talk to your victims before killing them?"

Blood Lance didn't like that. His lips compressed tightly and he turned away, moving off through the rain. Now that the war leader was gone, Cougar Time felt compelled to yank again on Ruff's tether, a little harder.

"You are a white man who plays Indian," Cougar Time said.

"Turn me loose. Let us see who is the man who plays."

"You are soft."

"Turn me loose," Ruff repeated. There was no answer this time. Ruff decided he wasn't going to be close friends with this one.

Glancing back, he saw that Wendy, mounted, was in good condition. Two warriors stood looking at her blond hair, but she only stared off into the distance, ignoring them. Jeff Warren was all right. Dried blood made a purple worm below his ear. He appeared only shocked to find himself looking into the brutal face of real violence.

Grover Suggs was stoical, but there was anger in his eyes. If they ever cut him loose, they were going to have their hands full. Dallas Shirke looked pleased with himself, puffed up like a banker living high on the farmers' money. Connolly, the one-eyed man, was looking back at Ruff as they rode out, not liking him any more than the Cheyenne, Cougar Time, apparently.

"You make friends wherever you go," Ruff told himself.

They rode out then through the rain, splashing across the narrow stream, leaving Carroll Chatsworth behind to sleep the long sleep that Blood Lance had planned for them all.

They wound through the trees and up over a sawtoothed divide. Now Justice could see the smoke from many fires, and as they emerged from the spruce and cedar forest, they found Blood Lance's camp.

"What MacEnroe would give to know where this is," Justice muttered.

Shirke heard him. "You'll not be telling anyone, will you, Justice?"

"Doesn't look like it. But you never know."

"Sure—you're the one with nine lives, isn't that so?"

"Me? One. One I try to live decently." Ruff looked at the bald man. "What's it like to kill your partner and steal his claim and then lure his kids out here so you can do the same to them? What's it like to be a pig bastard like you are, Shirke?"

Shirke went rigid and his arm lifted like a mechanical man's, his mouth twisting into a crooked grimace. A bit of saliva formed at the corner of his mouth and was washed away in the rain. The arm came down clubbing Ruff Justice on the neck, and Ruff fell from Hadji into the mud.

Cougar Time didn't wait for him to mount again. He rode on, dragging Ruff, who staggered and stumbled after him, the mud to his ankles despite the pines growing close around them. His head was swimming. He took a silent oath to keep his mouth shut.

The horse Cougar Time rode lifted its pace and Ruff was dragged headfirst for a hundred feet until with a mirthless smile the Cheyenne halted and let Ruff rise.

"I *will* have your hair," Ruff Justice told him then. "Now I mean it. I will have your hair and your spirit will be mine."

Cougar Time just sneered at him, but he didn't like the threat Ruff had made. Something deep in his somewhat superstitious mind rose up and waved threatening arms. He was afraid of losing his hair. All Indians are. He rode on, still leading Ruff, but he was a little more sober now. Once he showed Ruff his own scalping knife, and it was a fine one. Spanish steel, with elkhorn handles, narrow curved blade. It had been used. Ruff turned his head and spat.

"Didn't you hear them? I have nine lives. I'll see your hair on my leggings," Ruff Justice said.

He didn't believe it himself, but he tried to put enough force into his voice so that Cougar Time would think he did. It doesn't do to back down in front of an adversary. He just comes on then, pushing, shoving, taking. Let him think you have the tools even if you don't.

Justice even managed to laugh, and that tugged Cougar Time's mouth down. The Cheyenne looked at his scalping knife, and for a moment Justice thought the Indian was going to hurl himself at Ruff and take that long hair, the consequences be damned.

But he didn't. He put it away and rode on silently.

"You do get a little carried away, Mister Justice," Ruff told himself. "You definitely do."

"What's going to happen to us?" Wendy was speaking, not looking at Ruff but speaking to him. She clung to her saddlehorn with both hands. A Cheyenne had a lead rope tied to her horse's bridle.

"I don't know," Justice said honestly.

"They're going to kill us!"

"Settle down now," Ruff's voice grew soothing. "We'll get out all right."

Fortunately she didn't ask him how. They were nearly into the camp now. Ruff looked around, seeing no kids, no dogs, no women. It was a war camp, and although they had allowed themselves the luxury of their tepees, there were very few other items superfluous to the business of making war.

The Indians came out of their tepees or out of the trees to stand watching as the party of prisoners was led into the camp. Blood Lance was at their head, the whites under Shirke behind. The wind was cold. The rain had stopped and the sun was bright in Ruff Justice's eyes.

Ahead of them was a lodge twice the size of the others. Painted yellow, it had been decorated with snakes and sun symbols.

A man with fierce eyes came from the tepee. "What is this?"

"Prisoners, my brother," Blood Lance answered.

"What do I care? Kill them."

So that was White Badger, the brother of Blood

Lance. Ruff looked at him closely, noticing the tilt to his face, the way mouth and nose slanted away from each other. The eyes were warriorlike above high cheekbones.

"We must council," Blood Lance said, grabbing his brother's arm. The two Cheyenne stood looking into each other's eyes for a long minute before White Badger yanked his arm free and turned to walk back into the tepee.

"Are you going to kill them?" Ruff said to Blood Lance's back. There was no answer. The Cheyenne stood watching his brother's tepee. "Are you going to kill them—great warriors that they are? A boy and a woman! I can recall when the Cheyenne were brave and proud. Now they are cowardly."

Blood Lance whirled at that. "You"—a finger pointed at Ruff's eyes—"you will be silent or die first."

"Did you kill the little girl, too?" Ruff asked.

"What girl?"

"The white girl."

"I don't know what you mean."

"Sure you do. The one that was with the peace party—"

Shirke was beside Ruff now. "Shut up," he said.

"I don't understand you," Blood Lance said.

"Sure you do. The treaty party came looking for you, and you—"

Shirke lifted his rifle and the butt slammed down against Ruff Justice's skull. He went down facefirst in the mud, his head exploding with light and sound. Somewhere a woman screamed, somewhere a man laughed, and then he was tumbling through a velvet tunnel past the mocking masks with the throbbing eyes.

When he dared to open his own eyes again, it was

dark. Something smelled of bear grease. Opening his eyes cost him much pain. His skull wanted to split wide open and spill out Ruff's brains.

He lay still, testing his fingers and toes only to see if they worked. They did, but that small effort cost him pain. What had happened? Oh, yes, Shirke. Damn the man. But why?

Ruff saw a patch of deep-blue light. Stars dotted it. The sky appeared briefly and then was shut out as someone slipped into the tepee. He didn't move. He closed his eyes nearly completely so that the starlight wouldn't glint off it, should that happen again. His fingers meanwhile had slipped nearer the skinning knife that was sheathed inside his buckskin boot.

It was there still. He could feel the slender handle and then it was in his grasp.

The Indian was nearer now, but not near enough, moving from one side of the lodge to the other. It was utterly dark. It must have been very late, for outside nothing moved. What had happened to the others? Executed?

Maybe, but it seemed unlikely if they had kept Ruff alive. Right now his thoughts were focused on only one thing—the Indian near him. If he could kill that one silently and get out of the tepee, maybe cut his way out the back, well, there was always a chance—a very thin chance—that they could somehow escape.

The Cheyenne came a little nearer. He had only to grab him and prevent him from crying out. His head throbbed like mad. He bunched his muscles.

Suddenly Ruff's hand swept out and grabbed the Cheyenne's ankle and the Indian went down, Ruff leaping on top of him, already knowing that he couldn't do it, that he had made a mistake.

Because his searching hands found not the body

117

of a warrior but the body of a woman, quite young, lithe, and strong, yet not strong enough fend off the long-haired scout. He clamped his hand over her mouth and put the point of the skinning knife to her throat.

"Be still, woman. I don't want to kill you," he hissed, speaking in her own language.

Her eyes were wide, her breath hot against his hand. She shook her head from side to side.

"I mean to leave," he said. "Be quiet or you will make me hurt you. Do you understand?"

She didn't answer. He jabbed a little harder with the knife to convince her he wasn't kidding, then slowly he lifted his hand from her mouth, expecting a scream, a curse, a shout—Cheyenne women weren't easily cowed. Knife or none, she would fight.

But not this time. She lay on her back watching him with anxious eyes, her breasts rising and falling rapidly.

"Where are the other prisoners?" he asked.

"By the river. In the big trees."

"How many men are watching them?"

"I don't know. Two or three."

"Did the whites leave?"

"Shirke? He is here. With White Badger."

Then he asked the big question, "Where is the little white girl?"

She didn't answer for a time, too long a time.

Ruff gave her a shake. "Where is she?"

"No white girl."

"The hell there isn't. Answer me!"

"There is no white girl."

"Is she dead?"

"Yes," the woman said, "dead," but it seemed she said that only because she thought that was the answer Ruff Justice wanted.

Ruff released the woman. He stood and she stood too after a minute. "I'm going now. Find something for me to tie you up with."

"Wait." She placed a hand on Ruff's arm. "Aren't you the one who said something to my husband . . . something about the peace treaty?"

"Your husband?"

"Blood Lance."

So this was the half-Crow woman Blood Lance had married, the one who had dreamed of peace and asked him to sue for a treaty. Someone who would know what had gone wrong, why the Cheyenne war leader had turned his back on peace.

"I'm the one."

"There was a treaty?" she asked anxiously.

"Yes." He looked at her a moment too long and her hand fell away from his arm. "Of course there was."

"I thought so. I had hoped so."

She had turned her back on him. Ruff stood there indecisively. This was the time to try making his break, to tie the woman up and slip out into the night. Perhaps she would be a useful hostage; on the other hand, it seemed there was something to be gained here. Perhaps there was a road to peace, after all.

And she knew something about the white girl, about Marie. That was one thing Ruff would have bet on.

"That's where the girl came from," Ruff said. "There was a peace party on its way here. Carrying a treaty, gifts, and medicine." He had fallen into the Crow tongue and she turned back to study him with amazement. Ruff spoke all the Plains Indian languages, but only in the language of the Crow was he fluent. He had lived with them for a long while.

"I don't know what girl you mean," she answered, also in the Crow language.

"Yes you do. What happened? Is she dead?"

"I don't know what you mean. There was a peace party?"

"Yes."

"What happened?"

"You ought to know. They were massacred by Blood Lance in the big grove of trees below the pass."

"That is a lie!"

"Is it? Do you want to see the bodies? What is your name, woman?"

"Little Sky Bird."

"Little Sky Bird. All right. Little Sky Bird, how do they treat you here?"

"My husband treats me as his friend and his lover," she said defensively.

"You are Crow. Crow among the Cheyenne."

"Half-Crow."

"Half an enemy."

"I am not an enemy to my husband."

"No, but does he trust the Crow woman?"

Little Sky Bird stepped nearer. Angrily she said, "My husband trusts me, yes."

"He wouldn't lie to you, would he? Listen, Little Sky Bird, there was a peace party, it was attacked. The medicine for the pox was left behind. The other goods were stolen. I don't know what happened to the treaty. There was a little girl too, a little white girl named Marie, five years old, and she was taken away. I don't know what happened to her after that. Perhaps she too got the pox and died.

"This is the truth, all of it, and anything else you may have been told about the battle in the big grove of trees is a lie. What were you told?"

"My husband does not lie!"

"You think he doesn't. Perhaps he lied just this one time. Perhaps he lied so that you wouldn't know he never had any intention of doing what you had asked, of signing a peace with the whites."

"No," the voice from the tent flap said, "I did not lie. I do not lie to my wife." And Blood Lance, rifle in hand, stepped into the tent, his face dark and angry.

12

"BLOOD LANCE," Little Sky Bird said, and she started to rush to him before realizing—a warrior's wife always—that she would be in the line of fire if her husband decided to shoot. The rifle looked familiar. It should have. Justice had been carrying it for a long while. The big .56 Spencer had somehow never looked menacing to him, but it did now in Blood Lance's hands, hands that were wrapped tightly around it, the knuckles nearly white. The flap fell shut, and the moonlight and the gleam of starlight were shut out.

"How long have you been out there?" Ruff asked.

"A long while. I waited to shoot you when you came out."

"What's the matter? Couldn't you wait any longer?"

Blood Lance said, "I heard you. I listened and I heard what you told my wife. At first I could not believe any of it—all lies, I thought."

"And now?" Ruff asked.

Someone passed by outside. It wasn't much of a sound, but all three heard the whisper of moccasin leather against the earth.

Blood Lance tensed, waited until the sound had passed away, and then said, "Come with me. There are safer places."

Ruff agreed quickly, still not sure he had a handle on this. This man, this Blood Lance, was his enemy, was a murderer, a treacherous diplomat. Why, then, was he willing to talk to Ruff? There was something missing here and Justice meant to find out what it was.

Besides, it was his best way out of that camp. Not that Blood Lance had relaxed his vigilance. He stepped back and let his wife go out after whispering a word or two to her. Then he motioned for Ruff to follow. He still had a fair grip on that Spencer.

Outside, the moon glared through a screen of silver clouds. There were many stars, especially over the mountains, where it was clear as a bell.

"Which way?"

Blood Lance was distracted temporarily, looking around the camp, perhaps wondering who had been slipping around outside his tepee.

"Through the trees. You will see the path."

Ruff started that way, finding the break in the underbrush of scrub oak and blackthorn. Then he was into the pines, following a winding little path upward, toward a rocky outcropping where Little Sky Bird waited.

"There. Sit down so that I can watch you," Blood Lance said.

Ruff sat. The moon was bright on the ledge, the wind cool. The feathers stirred in Blood Lance's hair. He crouched down to stare at Ruff, the rifle across his knee.

"Tell me again, Justice. Tell me again what happened in the big trees."

Ruff did. Blood Lance watched him, trying perhaps to read truth or falsehood in his eyes. When Justice was through, he asked, "Why did you come here?"

"The girl. Her grandfather wants her back. He won't believe she is dead."

"He is a good man, this Spence?" Blood Lance asked.

"A good man, yes. A soldier who tried to become a peacemaker, who was working for the Indian."

Blood Lance nodded, not quite accepting that. He was silent for a time, and then, as if he had made a great decision, he shrugged and exhaled deeply.

"I will tell you what I know of this, Justice. You may not believe it all, but this is the truth."

"I'm listening."

"First of all, I am a warrior. My people need me to defend them. It has always been that way. Without warriors what would happen to the people? You understand that.

"Once my wife had a dream. When she has dreams, they are meaningful. This dream foretold our defeat if we fought on. Therefore, to fight on was not to defend my people but to betray them."

"I understand," Ruff said.

"Good. Do you dream, Justice?"

"Not in the way you mean, but I've known people who dream and know what will come."

"Yes. Then you understand this. I asked the whites for peace and they promised to make peace, but they said it would take much time. There is a place called Washington. All the treaties must go there, and if the men there have time, they will consider it. I know this. I have had newspapers given to me. I have learned to read English from picture books. One word at a time. Do you know why? So that I might protect my people."

"It seems you've done your best," Ruff replied. He was wondering if he knew this man at all. Who was Blood Lance?

"My brother did not want to sue for peace. White Badger said we must fight on to live free."

"You argued?"

"We argued, and my brother rode away. I found out only later why he wanted to fight on for a little while."

"Oh? I thought he just didn't trust the whites."

"That was what he told me. But it was the gold."

"What gold? Shirke's gold?"

"Yes, that gold. Shirke's gold."

"I don't follow this," Ruff said, but perhaps he was beginning to. Finally.

"White Badger fell in with Shirke. I don't know how they came to find each other, but they are two of a kind. My brother allowed Shirke to have the gold if Shirke would supply us with guns and bullets for them. There were other payments of goods. I don't know all that went on between them."

"That was why he wanted war," Little Sky Bird put in.

"What do you mean?"

Blood Lance took a slow breath, glanced at his wife, and answered for her. "There is much gold, very much. The word was bound to reach other whites, and they would come. White Badger didn't want others who might not give him guns and trade goods to come into the hills. Shirke agreed. He was paying much to have White Badger drive off anyone else who came."

"And then he paid your brother to kill his partner, Paddy Warren?"

"He did that for himself," Blood Lance said. "As I say, I learned this all only later. I was concerned with making my peace, White Badger with making his war. If I could have gotten a treaty in my hand to show the council leaders, then all of White Badger's excesses could have been halted. But the treaty did not come!"

"It came," Ruff said.

"That is what I heard you say tonight. At first I thought, That is a lie! But now I think that it may be the truth. Now I think of what my brother would have done if he heard that there would be peace instead of profit."

"Are you telling me White Badger massacred the Spence party, the doctor and his wife, the others?"

"Yes."

"They are telling it around that it was Blood Lance."

"Of course. What else would they tell?" Little Sky Bird said.

"You weren't there, you didn't know?"

"No, I swear it."

"What did your brother tell you?"

"That a band of whites had come and he had asked them to leave. They began to fight and so he fought back. That was all. They had many scalps."

"And a little girl?"

Blood Lance ignored the question, deliberately ignored it. "Where is the treaty?"

"Destroyed, I imagine."

"Perhaps not." Blood Lance was showing emotion now. He looked at his wife hopefully. "Perhaps it was not destroyed."

"It would have been, wouldn't it?" Ruff asked. "Shirke must have told your brother to make sure there was no peace, a peace that could take you onto a reservation and allow other whites to find his gold strike. Shirke would have told White Badger that it was imperative to find and destroy the treaty."

"I don't know. What if he could not find it, did not concern himself with it?"

"It seems a long shot."

"You were there. What did you find?"

"I wasn't looking for a treaty. I was looking for a little girl," Ruff reminded them.

"It could be there—so at least there is a chance."

"A chance?"

"A chance to save many lives, Ruff Justice. Yours, those of your friends, the lives of many, many people on the plains."

"All right. Let's have a look. Set the other whites free and we'll make our way back to the battlesite."

"I cannot set you free," Blood Lance said with some anguish. "I am war leader, but I can't act as if I were the tribal council."

"What do you mean?"

"I haven't the power to set you free."

"If we remain, White Badger will kill us. Or Shirke."

"Yes."

"You could prevent it."

"I cannot . . ."

Ruff had a suggestion, "You could let us escape."

"No. That is dangerous. You must go alone. Find the treaty, if it is there."

"And if it's not?" And that was more likely.

"Then ride on. I give you your freedom."

"I can't ride out without the others."

"But you must."

"I'd come back, Blood Lance. I'd come back and make my own small war."

Blood Lance just stared at him, not quite believing this mad white man. Then he said, "I think you would come back, no matter how many of us there are."

"You're right. What am I to do? Watch these other people slaughtered? What did they ever do to you except fail to pay tribute to your brother?"

"If we can find the treaty and show it to the council . . ."

"And how long will that take? How long will they wait before they execute Grover Suggs and the Warrens?"

"I don't know."

"This is war time. Your brother has the people demanding blood."

Blood Lance shook his head. "There is no way out."

"Release them. Or let us escape. Come with us to the battlefield. We'll look together."

"I have a wife, and a . . . My brother would retaliate."

"Then bring them along. Your wife. And the little girl."

"You know?" Little Sky Bird asked, her voice surprised.

"I know. Why don't you show her to me?"

"She's not here." The woman couldn't hold his gaze. She let her eyes slide away.

"Very well. I believe your lie."

"She is ours!" Little Sky Bird said vehemently. She stood, fists clenched, staring at Ruff challengingly. "We can have no children, don't you see? When Broken Nose, a friend, brought her to us, we took her in gladly. White Badger might have wanted to kill her for being white, but he didn't dare touch her."

"And she was a witness to the massacre. Didn't she tell you what happened?" Ruff demanded. "How could you believe White Badger's story when you had the girl? She must have told you what happened!"

Blood Lance spoke quietly. "She cannot speak, Ruff Justice. Cannot, will not . . ." He shrugged.

"She has said not a word in any language since she came to us."

"She has to go back."

"No!" Blood Lance was emphatic.

"Her grandfather has the right to have her. There she can speak, there she can grow strong."

"No, she is ours."

"And what will happen to her? You'll drag her around from place to place fighting a losing war, a war your dream told you you cannot win, until one day you are killed, both of you, or she is killed . . . No, it's no good, Blood Lance. The girl has to go back."

"No," Little Sky Bird said, and it was her final word. It was a pronouncement, not an argument. The child, her child, would not go away.

"I'm leaving," Ruff said. "And I'm taking the others with me. You can let me try and fail, or you can help me. Take a chance and go with me to the battlesite. If the treaty's there, as you think it must be, then you'll be able to come back and show it to the council, to stop the war."

"And if it is not?"

"Then you'll be an outcast from the tribe for taking our side, won't you? Then I reckon your brother will track you down and kill you if he can."

"Yes, he would."

"It's a risk. How much is peace worth to you, Blood Lance? How much are the lives of all your people worth?"

It was a long, long while before Blood Lance answered, and then not with words but with a gesture. He looked to his wife and then to the distant stars, toward the camp below, where warriors awaited the killing time.

Then very slowly, with ceremonial dignity, he handed Ruff Justice the big .56 Spencer rifle.

"Very well. It will be as you say."

"It must be."

"When?" Little Sky Bird did not argue. She had heard her husband's decision, and that was that. "When will this be done?"

It was Ruff Justice who answered. "Get the girl. It's time."

Then the woman was gone, slipping from the ledge through the thicket of scrub oak and manzanita below. Blood Lance waited only a moment longer. He, too, had made his decision, but it was a difficult one for him to carry out. It was traitorous to the tribe—it was also the only hope they had for finding peace ever.

The moon was too high, too bright, but they didn't have forever. "I am ready," Blood Lance said.

"We'll have to get the horses first."

"Yes. That won't be difficult."

"And getting the prisoners?"

Blood Lance nearly managed to smile. "*That* is not quite the same. There will be blood spilled, Ruff Justice, and I have no taste for it. It may be the blood of my own people."

"Even of your brother."

"Yes, that," Blood Lance said. "Even of my brother."

A brother who hadn't cared much for the tribe either, but only for filling his own pockets, for growing rich in trade goods and weapons. A brother who had deliberately sabotaged peace when it appeared peace might cost him his tribute.

"It may very well cost my brother's blood."

13

THE HORSES were herded together in the oaks beyond the camp. Ruff Justice and Blood Lance circled wide across the moonlit land, coming like two seeking shadows up from the long grass and into the trees. A horse blew and raised its head in anticipation and an owl lifted itself into the night sky on broad, slow wings.

"There!" Blood Lance whispered. A sentry sat with his blanket around his shoulders, leaning against a huge dead oak. He had his rifle on his lap. "And another across the clearing."

Ruff spotted that one too. He nodded to Blood Lance, who separated himself from Justice and walked right up to the guard, who rose.

"What is it, Blood Lance?"

"I want my pony, that is all."

"White Badger says no horses must leave tonight."

"My brother could not have meant me."

"He mentioned your name. Yours and Little Sky Bird's."

"Don't be foolish," Blood Lance said angrily. "What do you intend to do, keep your own war leader a prisoner?"

The guard didn't get a chance to answer. The man in buckskins had been moving nearer as the two

Cheyenne spoke. Now he detached himself from the shadows, and in three quick strides he was behind the Indian guard, clubbing him down with the barrel of his rifle. The man sank to the grass without a sound. Blood Lance picked up his rifle and tossed it aside.

He looked then at Ruff Justice, seeing something he had not seen before perhaps. He nodded and they continued silently on their way.

The second guard was an even simpler matter. He was half-asleep and Ruff administered a tap before the man had come fully awake. Well, maybe it wasn't exactly a tap. He went down and stayed there.

"Your horses are there," Blood Lance said. "I must take mine from the herd."

Ruff found the line where the captured horses had been tethered between two trees. He counted them up and came up with the right number. One extra. Carroll Chatsworth was gone, but his horse had been brought in.

And Hadji was there. That Ruff was some sort of rescuer, taking him back to where there were oats and corn and a dry stall, didn't occur to the black gelding. He viewed Ruff more as a snack, taking a nip at Justice's haunch.

There was no sign of the saddles anywhere, but all of the horses still wore bridle and bit. Ruff slipped onto Hadji's back, cut the tether with his skinning knife, and led the whole string out, feeling very antsy suddenly. He was in the middle of a Cheyenne camp and it wouldn't take much to wake up the whole Indian army.

He met Blood Lance a quarter of a mile away. He led a second horse. Conversing in sign language, they rode silently through the oaks, the horses' hoof-beats muffled by the rain-damp grass. Only Hadji blew, broke briefly into a sidestepping strut, and shook his head. The other horses were silent, ghostly. The moon was very low, shining dully through the oaks. Blood Lance found the spot and they swung down.

"How far?" Ruff asked, tying the horses.

"Very near."

Which suited Ruff. He didn't want to try outlegging a Cheyenne brave. They moved through the trees and suddenly they were there.

On the ground, which had been stripped of grass and packed down, the prisoners sat together. They were tied ankle to ankle, forming a circle. Around them stood three guards. One of them seemed to look directly at Ruff, to yawn and let his eyes shift away. It was enough to make the hair on the back of his neck stand up.

Blood Lance was tense, silent as the night breeze. He looked at Ruff and grimaced. It wasn't going to be that easy, but then they hadn't expected it would be. Still, it had to be done without shooting—had to be, or all hell was going to break loose.

If the men guarding the horses had been told about not letting Blood Lance take his pony, the odds were these braves had been told to be wary of him as well. White Badger had either guessed something or was taking no chances.

There wasn't much time. There were two men back there who were going to be waking up before too long. Blood Lance looked at Ruff and nodded. Time, whether they were ready or not.

Blood Lance cupped a hand to his mouth and made a sound like a quail. At first it didn't register with the guards, but then it did. Three heads turned toward the quail call.

"Look and see," Ruff heard one of them say, the one called Cougar Time, he thought.

"It's nothing."

"In the middle of the night? Fool. There could be a hundred Crow out there."

The younger warrior looked doubtful, but he finally shrugged and started into the trees. Blood Lance led him in, calling intermittently, softly, until the warrior was standing inches away from where Ruff lay in the underbrush.

Justice swept the warrior's feet from under him and leapt on him as he fell. One hand went over the brave's mouth, the other formed itself into a fist that crushed down into his jaw. Justice rose, grabbed his Spencer, and started at a trot after Blood Lance.

"Give me the rifle," the Cheyenne said when Justice caught up with him.

"No."

"You must give it to me. There is no other way."

Justice hesitated a long while. Had Blood Lance decided to back out of this while there was still time? Their eyes locked. Blood Lance's gaze was unreadable by starlight. His hand came up, asking for the Spencer.

"I give you my word, Justice. This is no trick."

Then, what could Ruff do? He had the man's word, and it meant a lot. Your word is a promise of honor. If you have no honor, you aren't even a man. He handed over the rifle.

"Go now. Into the camp," Blood Lance said. He turned Ruff bodily and started marching him forward.

The guards came to life as they saw Ruff and behind him Blood Lance with a rifle leveled at the white man's back. The prisoners came alert too, and Grover Suggs moaned a curse—perhaps he had been hoping that somehow Ruff could save them. Wendy hung her head. Her yellow hair was tousled, tangled. The kid was just scared, plain scared, his wide eyes following every motion.

Only Washta knew, seemed to know. His face was impassive, but there was a knowledge deep in his dark eyes.

"I found this one out there," Blood Lance said. "He had gotten away. He was trying to get his friends free."

"Where's Fire Eye?" Cougar Time asked. "We sent him to look."

"Justice overpowered him. Help me carry him back." To the other warrior he said, "Tie him with the rest of the whites."

Justice was seated roughly on the hard ground. The bond between the ankle of Jeff Warren and Washta was severed and Ruff was tied between them, using new lengths of rawhide. Justice was manhandled a little, but he didn't pay it any mind.

What did bother him was the descending moon; the dawn wasn't all that far away. He sat with his head hanging, as if defeated. Blood Lance and Cougar Time were going into the trees, with Blood Lance pointing out the way.

Justice glanced at the remaining guard, who was watching the other Cheyenne. Then he slipped the skinning knife from its sheath and cut the ties from his ankles, passing the blade next to Washta.

Jeff Warren's mouth was wide open, his eyes filled with terror at the idea of trying to escape from three armed Cheyenne Indians.

Washta cut his bonds and gave the knife to Suggs, slipping it across the small space between them neatly. The Indian guard glanced at them, saw nothing, and returned his gaze to the woods beyond.

Blood Lance reappeared.

"What's the matter?" the guard asked.

"We can't get him. Come on, we need your help."

"My help?" The guard was a little wary now.

"Yes, come on, you fool," Blood Lance said sharply.

The command started the Cheyenne into motion. He reached the woods and continued on. Ruff stood and cut the remaining ties free.

"They'll be back, Justice, for God's sake!" Jeff Warren said. "You'll get us all killed."

"They won't be back. Let's go. Or are you staying?"

"They'll . . ." The kid goggled at Ruff, toward the woods, and finally rose as if in a dream. Wendy had been tied tightly. Ruff had to help her stand up. The circulation had been cut off for a long while.

"Ruff," she whispered, "will it be all right?"

"Sure." He tilted her chin up and smiled. She accepted his answer, apparently. She wasn't stupid, but she needed to have something to cling to. Even an unlikely remark like that one.

It was a long way back—just a hell of a long way.

They waited until Blood Lance reappeared, frantically waving his arm, and they made a dash for the woods. The Cheyenne had three more rifles with him now. One for Suggs, one for the Crow Indian, who stood facing him, one for himself.

"What about mine?" Ruff asked.

Blood Lance nodded. They said no more to each other, but at that moment they reached an understanding: they were warriors committed to a common goal. Each could count on the other. To the hilt.

They moved off quickly through the trees, Ruff with Wendy holding his arm tightly. The horses were where they had left them—and already mounted on one of the Indian ponies was Little Sky Bird.

And the girl.

She was about five years old, dressed in buckskins, her dark hair neatly combed, decorated with beads. She looked out defiantly at a hostile, half-understood world.

Justice went to her. "Marie?"

"That is not her name," Little Sky Bird said sharply.

"The hell it's not."

"Not now. Now that is not her name."

"It's the name she was given when she was born. She'll have to keep it. Marie?"

But the girl wouldn't answer. She stared at Ruff, through him.

Blood Lance was mounted now. "Justice," he said, "we must be going!"

"Yes." Ruff looked at the girl a moment longer. "All right. Let's get the hell out of here."

For all of their urgency they couldn't run the horses. They had to walk them through the oaks, picking their way, watching the sky pale to the east, watching the night birds wing homeward.

Then they were onto the plains and still there had been no shouts behind them, no war cries, although they looked that way frequently, expecting White Badger to come.

They let the horses out. They ran on across the prairie into the face of the rising sun, knowing that a Cheyenne army was behind them now, knowing that the guards had been discovered, that the betrayal of Blood Lance had been found out, that now White Badger, in a rage, was screaming for his brother's death.

They would all be killed and there was only one way to stop it, and it was an unlikely chance. Find that damned treaty paper!

If it hadn't long ago been destroyed or taken or eaten by worms. Find that treaty! Show that White

Badger had deliberately sabotaged Blood Lance's peace.

Ahead, the land began to grow familiar. They weren't far from the battlesite. The oak grove began to lift from the plains, which were themselves shrouded in ground mist. And the first slender strand of pure gold appeared along the horizon. Dawn was racing across the plains toward them.

When they reached the battlefield, it didn't look much different than it had before, only a little more somber in the ground fog that continued to rise through the trees.

Blood Lance sat his pony for a long time, as if afraid to begin, to fail. Finally he swung down and Justice joined him. They began to search the ground again, to move around the burned wagons.

Washta had remembered. Washta went to the girl, the girl with the wide dark eyes, and he gave her the little forlorn doll he had found before. She looked at it, at him, and then she took it from him without a word, without expression.

"There's nothing," Jeff Warren said. "Why did we stop here? The Indians will be coming."

"This has to be done," Ruff answered.

Jeff was scared, his voice was a whine. "Maybe we can outrun them if we keep going! Stopping like this, we haven't a chance."

"What would it look like, Ruff?" Wendy asked. Her blouse was torn, her hair a mess, but she still looked beautiful this morning. Ruff hadn't taken the time to tell her that, there hadn't been the time. "Is the treaty just a piece of paper, or is it one of these fancy government documents with ribbons and seals? Is it engraved on stone?" Her voice was beginning to rise as the exhaustion and frustration set in.

"I don't know. Sorry," Ruff said, and his tone was

calm, soothing. He placed an arm around her shoulders. "Just keep looking."

"Looking where?" She poked at her hair with nervous fingers. "I've been all through those clothes, through the foodstuffs and medicine boxes."

"I don't know where. Somewhere we haven't thought of," Ruff said.

"I . . ." The voice was a tiny peep. A creaking, scratchy thing, a long-unused, immature voice. Ruff whirled to see Marie Spence, holding the doll by one arm, walking to him. Her eyes were wide. "I know where. The paper Grandfather . . ."

"Yes?"

"Father and Mother and Grandfather . . ."

Ruff knelt down. "Marie, listen. Your grandfather is waiting for you."

"He's dead, like Mother and Father are dead."

"No, he's not."

"They told me."

"I don't care what they told you, he's not dead. I saw him in Bismarck a few days ago. He sent me to look for you. He wants you home again—and if you'll tell us where that paper is, then we can ride on down there and you can be with him again."

Ruff looked across the girl's shoulder at Little Sky Bird, who turned away from him, her mouth drawn down in anguish. Ruff held Marie's arms and looked into her eyes. "Do you know where it is?"

"Will you take me to Grandfather? You promise that?"

"Yes," Ruff said, "I do."

"It's where the Indians threw it," she said at last.

"Where is that?"

"When we rode away. We stopped and one of them threw it away."

"*Where?*"

"Over there. In the stream." She lifted an arm and pointed, and Ruff felt his heart sink. He looked at Blood Lance and saw the disappointment on the Cheyenne's face. If they had thrown the treaty in the stream all those months ago, there wasn't a damn thing left of it now. It had floated away or been covered by silt or rotted to nothing. Still, they could look.

"Show me where," Ruff said.

"For God's sake, Justice," Jeff Warren shrieked. "They'll be coming after us! We've got to ride. You heard her. What could be left of it?"

"We'll look and see."

"Justice"—there were tears in the kid's eyes—"they'll be coming."

"Not for a while."

But he was wrong there. Washta was standing looking westward through the trees and with dismay he turned to Ruff Justice and he said, "They come now, Ruffin. I can see the horses, many horses. White Badger is coming now."

14

JEFF WARREN let out a little shuddering groan of despair. Wendy put her hand to her mouth and turned to face the west. Grover Suggs spat eloquently. Blood Lance was stoical. What was there to be done?

"We were free," Jeffrey Warren said, grabbing at Ruff's shirt. "We had it made. We could have beaten them back to Valdez's trading post. But you had to stop! You had to stop and look for that damned meaningless treaty!"

Ruff clawed the kid's fingers off his shirt. When he spoke, his voice was brittle, icy.

"You go on. Get out of here. There's time, you ride."

"I can't . . . You mean, alone?"

"Go on!" Justice roared.

"I . . ." All words escaped the kid. He just stood there, tears streaming down his cheeks.

Wendy Warren said, "Be a man," and turned away, her cheeks burning with shame.

"Let's go," Ruff said. "Marie, are you ready to show us the place now?"

"Yes."

"Good. Let's have us a look and then we'll get on out of here and see Grandfather again."

Ruff tried to keep it light for the kid, but even she must have known the seriousness of their situation.

Now through the gaps in the trees they could all see horsemen. Still far off, but coming fast. When they reached the stream, Marie just stood there. That was all, just stood there.

"Come on, honey," Ruff coaxed.

"I don't know."

"You have to know," he said quietly. "Try to remember. Think."

"Over there, I think. Yes, we crossed the river. I was with a big man. The others wanted to make me dead like Mother and Father, but he held me and they didn't do it."

"And where were the other men?" Now Ruff could hear the horses out on the prairie, the onrushing army of White Badger.

"There." A diminutive finger poked toward a ford farther on.

They started that way hurriedly, Little Sky Bird holding Marie's hand, clinging to her yet, but in a way that was no longer motherly somehow.

"Right there," the girl said. "And it landed out there somewhere."

Ruff was into the water, which was to midcalf, icy. The bottom was gravel, which was fortuitous. No silt to cover up items dropped or thrown there, a firmer surface into which heavier objects wouldn't sink.

But they were looking for a piece of paper—only a piece of paper. Ruff called to the shore, "Marie, was it in anything, the treaty?"

"A box, I think. A tin box."

Ruff's heart quickened with the small hope. There was a chance, a small chance. But the river was a living, shifting thing, whimsical and changeable. The recent rains could have brought a strong-enough current to carry away anything. And if it had been carried away . . . Ruff's eyes drifted downstream to

142

where the river eddied and swirled toward a snag of fallen trees and driftwood. He started that way at a near run, water splashing up.

The Cheyenne were less than a mile off now. A war cry drifted eeriy toward them. No one raised a weapon or tried to run. What was the use in that?

"What are you doing?" Wendy was there suddenly, her blouse soaked through with water, her eyes shining with excitement. "This is madness!"

Justice continued to wade through the shallow water. She clutched at his arm, but he knocked her away. Glancing over his shoulder, he saw White Badger's people reach the river and drive their ponies downstream toward Blood Lance, who stood stock-still, the wind shifting his feathers, his rifle hanging loosely from his hand. A dozen steps away was Little Sky Bird, holding Marie, who clutched her doll. Washta, Jeff Warren, and Grover Suggs stood in a group just behind her.

"Ruff! We have to at least try to fight, to talk our way out of this!" Wendy Warren lifted her skirt and stepped toward him, tripping. She went down and rose again, sputtering, choking. Ruff ignored it all.

White Badger was closing the distance now. He was fifty yards upstream. Still Blood Lance simply watched. Wendy had stopped her pursuit of Ruff and stood quietly herself, soaking wet, staring at the approach of the painted Cheyenne.

Only Ruff Justice moved. He bent down and then dived under, rising again, turning this way and that. *Madness.* It was madness. He was performing some sort of strange individual ritual, some crazy baptism. The water was icy, quick-running. He dived under again. And again.

White Badger had stopped before his brother. His horse tossed its head and blew. Blood Lance stood there immobile, expressionless. "You"—White Badger's finger was leveled—"traitor, brother. You must die on this morning. Now."

"Traitor? You can call me that? One who sold his people's peace for the white man's goods?"

White Badger rode nearer. He kicked out suddenly, his moccasined foot striking the point of Blood Lance's chin. The Cheyenne war leader was knocked backward to splash into the water. Little Sky Bird cried out. Blood Lance, sitting in the stream, shook his head and rose.

"You are the traitor, my brother," Blood Lance said. Blood ran from his mouth and from his nostrils. "You know it. You know what was done here. The council members should know."

"Know what?" White Badger laughed and waved a hand carelessly. "What happened here? I have told everyone how it was."

"And you lied."

"You would call me—" White Badger's rifle came up.

Blood Lance still stood in front of it, unflinchingly. "There was a party of whites here who were bringing medicine for the terrible pox and gifts for our people. They also had a treaty, the treaty I had asked for. You came with a few of your dog soldiers and killed them all—except the little girl. One man at least was strong enough to prevent her murder."

"What is this madness? Where is this treaty? Who saw this act you describe? What is it—another of your Crow wife's mad dreams?"

"It is no dream." Blood Lance looked to the council members among the riders, men who made the laws and had the power to give life or proclaim death. "You, Blue Fox; you, Far Eagle—you must listen to me. You must not let my brother kill me in

144

cold blood, you must not let him assume my mantle. To do so is to send our people to their death!"

Blue Fox, who was almost as old as Washta, but limber and alert, asked, "But why did you run away? Why did you free the white prisoners, Blood Lance? Then you were not concerned with waiting for a council decision. As your brother says, who saw this massacre? I understood it was a fight between interlopers and the warriors of our clan under White Badger. Why did you not challenge your brother's word before? Why now, when it seems you use this to confuse matters because you are accused."

"I only recently discovered—"

"How did you discover it? A white told you?"

"*Yes*." Blood Lance's fists were clenched and held to his chest.

"What would the whites be expected to say? They have tricked you. We all know you were mad for this treaty you sought."

"But they *had* the treaty!"

"Then, where," White Badger asked smugly, "is it?"

There was no answer. The river ran past and the wind ruffled the leaves of the giant oaks in the grove behind them.

"It's here," a voice said finally. All eyes went to the white man in buckskins who was walking toward them, holding aloft a tin box. "*Here* is the treaty. Where White Badger threw it."

"Lies!" White Badger's rifle came up, but Blue Fox pushed the barrel back down.

Ruff approached the Cheyenne with his heart thudding dully. The wind was cold on his soaking-wet body. His teeth chattered. He held the tin box overhead with both hands. His long, dark hair was in his

145

face. White Badger was watching him with dark, threatening eyes.

Crazy, Justice, he told himself. What the hell made anyone think that the treaty inside that tin box would even be legible after this time? Yet, here he was marching up to the Cheyenne chiefs with the box like some sacred tablet discovered in the silver river.

"Here is the treaty. The treaty White Badger killed for. The treaty he hurled away so that his treachery wouldn't be discovered, the treaty that Blood Lance fought for—honorably fought for—so that his people could live with security and honor in peace."

White Badger's face contorted. He started to say something, but his jaw didn't seem to be working properly. Blood Lance had turned to watch Ruff's approach. The eyes of the council members and of all the Cheyenne were on Justice, who came forward with that tin box elevated.

White Badger's rifle came up again and Ruff saw it. He flung himself to one side as the Winchester cracked. The bullet slammed into the tin box, narrowly missing Ruff's head as he dived into the river. From the bank an answering shot came. Washta fired once and his bullet penetrated White Badger's skull, just before the ear, blowing the warrior from his pony to land in the stream and stain the silver water with his blood.

The Cheyenne started to fire back, but Blue Fox's hand went up and a sharp command stayed them. The council chief got down and went to examine White Badger's body. He knelt and then looked at Washta.

When he spoke, he said, "White Badger admits the lie." He looked for one of White Badger's lieutenants and found Cougar Time among the painted warriors he had with him. The old chief rose and said, "I ask you once—what is the truth, Cougar Time?"

The brave hung his head slightly. "It is as Blood Lance says," he answered. "White Badger knew the peace treaty was on its way to our camp. The white, Shirke, told him."

"So." The old man nodded. "So, that is that. Find your pony, Blood Lance. We must ride home now."

"Yes. I will find my pony and follow you."

Ruff Justice walked to them and he stood there in knee-deep water watching the old chief. No one said a thing. There was nothing to speak about. Ruff gave the tin box to Blood Lance and waded to the shore. He waited there for Wendy Warren, who came—water-soaked, cold, happy, laughing—and kissed his mouth and clung to him as the Cheyenne war party, leaving White Badger where he lay, turned and slowly made their way homeward.

Blood Lance was opening the tin box with his knife. When the latch gave and it creaked open, they found nothing but a soggy wad of parchment paper, a few ounces of sediment.

"It wasn't there!" Jeff Warren said, sagging a little.

"Didn't think there'd be much," Ruff Justice said. He stood shivering, his arm around Wendy.

"Then why . . . ?"

"Well, there was a chance. And we didn't have any other. Fortunately White Badger didn't have the nerve to find out what was in the box. His guilt got the better of him. And Washta sent him home."

"We have no treaty now," Blood Lance said.

"Sure. At least I think so. The treaty is a law, Blood Lance. The paper only says what the law will be. You can destroy the paper but not the law. "

"I must have the paper," Blood Lance said.

"You don't trust them still?"

"No. Would you?"

"No," Ruff said honestly. "Well, a copy of the treaty shouldn't be hard to come by, though it may take a while. You send someone in or come yourself to Fort Lincoln. Find yourself an Indian agent you can trust."

"Like you, Justice?"

"Not me, no. I had a job like that once. The Indians wouldn't trust me and the white bureaucracy wouldn't support me. It was frustrating and damned lonesome. But there are people suited to the job, and good at it. I've met a few."

"For now I must go home," Blood Lance said. "The council must understand all of this completely."

"I know that. I'll be waiting, hoping to hear good things about the treaty."

"Thank you for that, Justice." Blood Lance looked at his wife, who still stood holding Marie's small hand. "The girl . . ."

"The girl's going home," Ruff said.

"Home to . . ."

"Home to her grandfather." Ruff added, "If she wants to go. I think she does. You did right by her, you and Little Sky Bird. You took her in and treated her like your own, but she's not, and she never would be. Maybe you'll find a Cheyenne girl to adopt, maybe you'll yet have your own child. But if Marie wants to go home, I'm taking her."

"Marie?" Blood Lance asked, the name strange on his lips.

"I want my grandfather," she said, and she ran to Ruff. She ran, but she stopped within three strides of him and rushed back to cling to Little Sky Bird, allowing herself to be picked up and hugged and stroked as they both wept.

Then Little Sky Bird put her down and Marie walked to Ruff, dragging the doll.

She stood with Justice as Blood Lance and his wife recovered their ponies and Jeff and Suggs brought Hadji and the other horses to the creek. Once Blood Lance was mounted, he had to bend down to take Ruff's hand. Briefly he squeezed it and then he and Little Sky Bird, who did not look back, rode across the river and out of their lives. The little girl waved for a long while.

"I'm freezing," Wendy said.

Ruff wrapped an arm around her. She was shivering still. The sun was rising but the wind was keeping the temperature down.

Washta looked to Ruff. "We ride now, Ruffin?"

"We'd better."

"Can't we stay and dry out?" Wendy asked, turning green eyes on Ruff.

"No. Let's ride on," he answered.

"But why?"

"Let's just do it." He kissed her briefly. "Okay?"

"Yes," she answered a little put out. "Whatever you say."

"Thank God it's all over," Jeff Warren said. Ruff Justice, who had no such idea, turned toward Jeff, frowning. "I don't suppose we can work that claim now. Maybe after they're on the reservation, right? But just to get out of here with our lives!" The three older men were still watching him silently. "What's the matter?"

"It's not over yet," Grover Suggs said. "Is it, Justice?"

"No. Not yet."

"What do you mean?" Jeffrey Warren laughed uneasily. "They've all turned back. They won't be back. The Cheyenne have gone home."

"Yes," Ruff answered, "the Cheyenne have."

"Then what are you talking about?"

"Shirke. Shirke and eight armed men."

"Shirke? But—"

"Don't be a fool," Grover Suggs said sharply, surprising Jeff. "Do you think the man can let us ride back to Bismarck with what we know? He murdered his partner, your father. He sold or gave guns to the Indians. He gave instructions for the peace party to be attacked! Do you think he can afford to let us live now?"

Jeffrey Warren had gone pale again. He stood staring at Suggs, his lips slightly parted, the wind shifting his pale, thin hair. No, he hadn't thought of that. Not of Shirke. Now the fear that had gone with the Indians came back with a rush. A cold, gnawing fear it was that settled in his gut and made his insides ache. He asked Ruff Justice, "What do we do?"

"Ride."

15

THEY HADN'T SEEN Dallas Shirke all day, but they knew he was back there somewhere, had to be. He couldn't let them go, so he would kill them, every one, the woman and child included.

They didn't have anything to eat that night. The saddlebags had gone with the saddles, lost in the Cheyenne camp. Stomachs shrunk and protested loudly. The moon rose and the long plains were silvered. The hills surrounding the cold camp were dark, undulating softly, nearly grassless, treeless.

Wendy Warren found Ruff Justice a little way from camp. He stood there, arms folded, watching the land to the north. She took his arm as she stepped up beside him. His head didn't even turn.

"What is it?" she asked.

"Just thinking."

"Any good coming of it?"

"Not so's you'd notice." He turned and put his hands on her shoulders. "Are you all right?"

She laughed briefly, softly. It was a pleasant sound, Ruff Justice decided. "All right, after riding out here on a nightmare, being taken captive by the Indians, threatened with death, soaked through, baked by the sun, half-starving to death . . ." She laughed again. "Yes, yes, I guess I am all right. Thanks to you."

"To me?"

"For being along. For cushioning here and there, for pulling us out when it really got tough."

"Luck." Ruff shrugged.

"Men like you have a lot of luck. You make it because you know what you're doing; you're competent and you know just who you are. You fit your world exactly."

"Maybe, maybe not." Ruff shrugged again, as if it were of no importance or as if his thoughts were so far away that he really couldn't concern himself with the conversation. Maybe it was some of each.

"Sure! Look at my brother. He's a good strong young man, but this isn't his kind of world, his sort of place. He can't handle it."

"Can you?"

"You mean, am I going to worry about coming back and working that claim? Maybe. After everything is settled with the Indians. But no, I don't belong here either, Ruff. If I came back, it would just be for a time, for long enough to get things organized, to go bust or prosper with that claim. Then it would be back East, home."

"Uh-huh," Ruff said distractedly.

Wendy smiled and touched a finger to his upper lip, tracing his mustache. "They really are worrying you, aren't they?"

"You'd better believe it," Ruff answered. "We can't fight 'em off, I don't think. I don't think we can beat 'em to Valdez's, let alone the fort or Bismarck."

"We'll be all right."

"Keep saying it," Ruff replied.

"I will. I'll make you believe it, too. What you need to do now is relax, get your mind off it for a bit— think about something too long and the mind just starts going in circles, doesn't it?"

"It does." Ruff gathered her to him and held her a little more tightly. "What did you have in mind for relaxing me, for getting my mind off of the Shirke gang?"

"What did you think?" she asked, tilting her head to one side. The moonlight made an aureole around her golden hair.

"You going to make me guess?" He kissed her then, deeply, and she sagged against him.

"No," she managed to breathe when he was finished. Then she took his hand. "Come on," she urged.

"Where?"

"I don't care. Here? I saw a little hollow back this way, on the side of the hill."

She was in a bit of a hurry, it seemed, tugging at Ruff as she walked back along the dark trail to the hill slope and then up, slipping twice before they reached the hollow that overlooked their own camp and the plains for miles.

Ruff stood watching the night and the distances. "Nice view," he said dispassionately. Wendy was meanwhile fussing with her buttons and hooks, cursing under her breath, small, feminine curses. "I'm glad you brought me up here—I can see for a good long way," he teased.

"Damn you," she said, and then she rushed to him, naked, lithe, and warm, and she pressed herself to Ruff Justice, wrapping her arms around his neck, her lips seeking his.

Her grip loosened and she sank to her knees before him, her fingers going to the fly of his trousers. With some difficulty she opened them and Ruff sprang free to be encased in her hand. Her cheek was against his thigh, her breath was warm and soft.

"Please. Hurry," she said, and Ruff finished undressing. She was on the ground on a bed made of

153

her clothing, watching him as he came to her by moonlight. She rolled onto hands and knees, and Justice eased up behind her. Her grasping fingers reached back, found him, and guided him in.

She was warm and eager, her body anxious for his. She cupped his sack, holding it against her as Ruff's hands roamed her smooth, curved buttocks and reached forward to find her breasts.

He felt her quiver beneath him and he began to sway against her, to drive it in slowly, methodically. The moon was on her flesh, glossing it. Her face was concealed behind her mass of loose golden hair. Her hands held him to her heated body, as if she were afraid he would leave her too soon.

He had no intention of doing that. Wiping back his hair, he knelt erect, resting his palms on her smooth, flawless ass, watching as his shaft entered her and then withdrew, teasing her, bringing her to life.

He heard her gasp, felt her body alter and soften, felt the hand that held him begin to urge him to a climax as she went slack and then tense, rocking against Ruff, not wanting him to hold back, not able to do so herself.

Then quickly, before she really noticed, Ruff turned her, placing her flat on her back. His lips went to her breasts, to her throat, and then he lay against her, feeling the heat of her body, the urgency of it as her hands went behind him, gripped his buttocks, and pulled him to her, her cadenced urgings growing quicker as her head rolled from side to side and a series of small puffing gasps escaped her lips.

"Just a little more," she breathed into his ear. She bit at the lobe and her breath caught. "Oh, just a . . . Now, please, Justice. And her fingers dug into his bare back, her body writhed beneath his, her legs spreading until it seemed they would tear as she reached a driving climax, bringing Ruff to his own completion simultaneously.

She lay back then, breathing in and out slowly, deeply, stroking his back with her fingernails, running down his spine, then up, under his long hair to the nape of his neck, then down again endlessly as if that was all it would take to keep her satisfied forever—that and the presence of Ruff within her, next to her, his hard knowing body a part of hers.

It was midnight when he rose. The night was cool. He covered her with her skirt to keep her warm, but she was awake and she sat up, staring at him from out of a muzzy dream. Her blond hair was in a tangle. Her breasts were free of clothing, proud and resilient, round and perfect. Her legs were slightly spread, her toes pointing up to the starry night sky.

"Where are you going?" she asked.

Ruff stepped into his trousers. "Riding out."

"Riding out?" She shook her head in confusion. "Without me . . . without any of us?"

"That's right."

"But why?" She started to rise and then changed her mind, as if the night's exertions hadn't left her with enough strength to make it.

Ruff was tugging his shirt on now. "In the morning—start at first light—you people ride south. Ride hard. You keep Marie with you all the time. Ride for Tom Valdez's trading post. And *stay* there. Sooner or later an army patrol will swing past. Then you can travel with them back to Lincoln."

"But you? I don't understand this," she said with the gnawing fear that she *did* understand it. "What are you going to do, Ruff Justice?"

"Me? I'm going hunting."

"Meat?"

155

"Yes. Shirke."

"No, Ruff!" Now she was on her feet, in his arms. "You said we couldn't beat them, that it wasn't possible."

"*We* couldn't. Maybe I can. I can sure as hell slow them down anyway. You ride south and I'll be behind you, keeping them off your tail."

"If they catch you . . ."

"They won't."

". . . they'll kill you, Ruff, kill you horribly."

"They won't catch me." Justice kissed her briefly, gingerly almost, and then pried her fingers from his shoulders. "It'll be all right. Take my word for it." He grinned. "A man like me, I make my own luck, remember? I fit this situation, this world exactly."

"No you don't." She backed away from him. "Nobody does—not this horrible, stinking world!" She snatched up her clothes and stood hunched forward, staring at him. "You're going to go out and get yourself killed and you don't even care about anyone else!"

There were tears in her eyes and she wiped them away savagely. She started to say something else and then just gave it up. In a fury she stormed away, sliding and stumbling down the hill, until the night shadows had swallowed her up.

"You're wrong, lady," Ruff Justice said. "I do care. About you and everyone else. This is the only way I know to do this, that's all."

And then he forced his thoughts away from Wendy Warren and onto the future, to the job at hand, to Dallas Shirke and his band of cutthroats, some of whom would have to pay the price, the price as announced by the .56 Spencer rifle Ruff Justice would be carrying north with him.

He had told Wendy to make sure they rode out at

first light. Ruff didn't intend to wait that long. He was going while darkness covered his movements. He found Hadji in the darkness and slipped the picket line, getting up on the black gelding's back. There wasn't much foolishness in Hadji on this night. Maybe he was tired.

Or maybe he sensed that Ruff Justice meant business.

The moon had passed its zenith and was sliding down toward the far mountains.

An hour later it was down after glowing orange for a brief moment, hanging huge and misshapen above the far peaks. Then it grew dark. The stars were large and silver in a deep-velvet sky, but their light never seemed to touch the dark earth.

Hadji ambled on, his stride smooth and sure.

"Hold up," Ruff said under his breath, and he halted the big black, looking around slowly, his eyes alert. Then in the darkness the tall man smiled.

"I think we've found us some bad men, Hadji," Ruff said, and he patted the black's neck. Hadji tried to bite him.

Ruff started forward again, veering westward, away from the trail they had followed earlier. For there was someone else on that trail now, or rather camped near it. Someone he wanted badly to meet. But they couldn't be allowed to see him first. Rules of the game.

Justice knew they were there because the scent was still on the night air. The fire was dead, put out long ago, but still the smell of dead fire, of ashes, drifted through the night where no other smells could conceal it. It stood out sharply among the mingled, pungent scents of sage and greasewood.

It was man smell and the stalking wolf stayed clear of it, the fox and the coyote. But it drew other men

157

to it. It called man the hunter irresistibly. And man the hunter was Ruff Justice.

He moved toward the camp from the west, carrying no true anger but only a deep feeling that the job ahead of him was essential, that other, better lives depended on him doing this thing properly.

He still couldn't see the camp. He dismounted, however, on the chance that Shirke would have guards posted. It was difficult to see why he would bother. He couldn't have believed that the fleeing men ahead of him would turn and attack his larger force.

But Shirke had been around awhile. He was cunning and knew how to survive in a land where the biggest dog wins. It was possible.

Ruff left Hadji ground-tethered and made his way to the crest of the low knoll ahead of him. From there he could see a fair distance across the starlit prairie. But he couldn't see the camp. He knew it was there, very close, but he couldn't pick it out. He slowly let his eyes sweep the skyline, the other hills for a possible picket, but he saw nothing. The scent of fire was still there, very clear, very near.

And then, from below, a horse nickered and Ruff smiled again. It was a tight, wolfish expression. His hand involuntarily tightened on the rifle he carried. He only hoped Hadji, in the draw behind him, didn't answer the horse in Shirke's camp. But Hadji was above such trivial matters. He was silent. Justice began to move forward, down the hill slope toward the sleeping camp somewhere below.

The brush grew heavier and he moved through it with difficulty, cursing softly as a rock rolled from under foot and rang off another below.

The air was rich with the scent of sage, chia, sumac. He held his rifle high and waded through one particularly thick tangle of brush.

And then he was there quite suddenly, looking down into the camp of Dallas Shirke. They all seemed to be asleep, disproving the notion people have about guilty consciences. Nothing disturbed their rest. They were babes in their mothers' arms. Vicious little babes who killed as a way of life.

Some of them wouldn't be doing that much longer.

Justice wanted the horses first—if he could get them. The idea was to give Wendy, Suggs, and the kid time enough to reach Valdez's post. Taking Shirke's horses would assure them of that time.

If it could be done.

At least one of those horses was a little antsy. It nickered again as Ruff crept nearer, moving in a crouch, his rifle held low and ready. A man loomed up before him suddenly and instinct alone saved Justice.

He looped the butt of the Spencer through the air and it tagged the guard at the base of the skull, beneath his ear, and he went down without a sound. Ruff moved in and searched the man. He slipped his revolver from him, tossed his rifle aside into the heavier brush, and then dragged the unconscious man that way as well.

He was panting when he finished that, reclimbed the little knoll, and moved in a half-circle toward the horses that he had spotted against the plains.

They were a shifting, many-headed shadow against the deeper darkness beyond. Ruff saw starlight gleam on an eye, saw a horse shake its head, mane swirling.

Then that damned nervous pony whickered again and all hell broke loose.

16

THE HORSE whinnied and the sound of alarm was echoed by another horse. Ruff hit the ground, but he was just too slow. There had been a second man standing watch, one Ruff hadn't been able to pick out from behind the boulders where he stood. At the sounds from the horses he had stepped out, seen Ruff drop to the ground, and opened fire.

His rifle lashed flame at Ruff and a near bullet plowed up grass beside Justice's elbow. Ruff pulled the trigger of the big Spencer and it bucked against his shoulder as the five-hundred-grain bullet smoked out of the barrel of the buffalo gun and tagged the outlaw in the center of the chest, hurling him back as if he had been yanked by an invisible puppeteer.

Ruff was to his feet, cutting through the line holding Shirke's horses, flagging them away with his hands, chasing them onto the prairie. He yelled and whistled, and frightened of night spooks, they kept running.

"There he is!"

The cry was from behind Ruff and to his left. He threw himself to the ground to roll to one side as three bullets sang past him, ricocheting off the boulders behind and beside him.

Ruff answered with the Spencer, sending four shots into the silhouettes the outlaws presented. One of them screamed out with horrible pain; another dropped to the earth and tried to drag himself away. But there were more guns firing now. A hail of bullets kept Ruff low, unable to pick a target or return their fire.

He drew his legs under him now, waited until there was a short pause as the outlaws debated their course of action, then dashed for the boulders, drawing a storm of gunfire.

He didn't halt once he reached the shelter of the big rocks, but kept on moving, knowing they had only one thought in mind now: kill Ruff Justice. He made a run for the deep brush higher up the slope and might have made it unseen but the guard he had cold-cocked earlier had come alert, and as Ruff rushed toward him out of the darkness, he shouted out.

"Hey! Stranger in the camp!"

Which was something the others already knew, but it served to focus the pursuit, and as Ruff hit the brush, the guns opened up again and he was forced to the ground once more to slither upslope, bathed in his own sweat now despite the coolness of evening.

Hadji was what he wanted, to be on the big black's back and riding free. It would take some time for Shirke to round up his horses, maybe time enough.

Ruff was breathing through his mouth raggedly as he crested the knoll. He could see the outlaws working their way through the brush now, an occasional grunt or curse reaching him as a man slipped and knocked his knee on a stone or took a stick in the face.

They knew where he was, so there was no point in playing dead. Ruff placed the curved butt of the Spencer to his shoulder, tracked a target, and squeezed off. Flame spewed from the muzzle of the big gun and his target went down writhing and cursing in the brush. The others beat a hasty temporary retreat, but not before Justice put a round into the leg of another Shirke man. That one was lucky. The shock of a bullet like that striking a limb is enough to kill. But the .56 slug literally just grazed him, snipping open his trouser leg and digging a groove in the thigh.

He went down, not seriously hurt, but scared and in pain.

Ruff started on, trying to calculate how many Shirke men were left, not coming to a certain conclusion. The Spencer was empty. His spare ammunition was in his saddlebags back at Frenchman's Pass, leaving him only the Colt he had lifted from the Shirke man below and the rounds the bandit had had in his gun belt.

Hadji was in the draw just below him, and hearing more shouts from behind, Ruff slid, slipped, ran, and skidded down the hill through the thinning brush toward the big black horse.

He leapt across a small stony ravine and started at a dogtrot toward the gelding, now only a few hundred feet away.

He reached the spot where he had left the black and stood looking around in disbelief. Hadji was gone! Justice wiped the hair from his eyes and took a second look. Then he started on again, his blood boiling. If he didn't find that horse, it changed the game completely. But where was the damned ornery nag?

A rifle from behind kept Justice moving. At first he wondered how they were coming so close with conditions like they were. It wasn't tough to figure after he realized the sky was paling in the east and the sun was on its way.

"Terrific," he muttered through his ragged breath. "You did good, Justice. Trusted everything to a devil horse that does just as he pleases whenever he pleases."

He swore he'd get rid of the black. He would trade it for a little spotted pony, a three-legged mare. "How are you going to do that, son? You seriously think you're going to get out of here alive?"

By now Shirke was probably closer to his horses than Justice was to Hadji. He looked to the sky across his right shoulder. Lighter yet, definitely lighter. There seemed to be a thread of deep crimson higher up.

The rifle from behind spoke again and the bullet, though not near enough to be a threat to Ruff's life, was enough to keep him moving. He hated to do it, but he ditched the Spencer. An empty rifle wasn't quite what he needed just then. What he needed was a damned horse!

He dipped down into a sandy coulee where willow brush grew among broken gray cottonwoods and bluffs twenty feet high rose up on either side. It was cool in the bottom. Ruff startled a feeding cottontail and it took off at a speed he envied.

The rifleman fired again despite the cover of the willows, and it was a near thing. Ruff glanced up, seeing the horseman against the gray sky, seeing the rifle in his hands. He dived for the ground again as a second shot was fired.

"I'll kill that horse. I've never beat a horse, but I'll beat him to within an inch of his life. And then some." Ruff wriggled through the willows. He considered stopping, throwing some lead back at the sniper above, but that short-barreled Colt was just going to spray bullets all over the countryside. A hit would be a stroke of amazing luck. He would have to wait until he was nearer, if he lasted that long ... Another shot.

Now Justice, on his feet again, winding along the bottom, got his first fair look at the hunter above him. The bald head showed clearly. He could see a half of his face by the new sun.

Dallas Shirke. Shirke, and he must have been laughing himself silly. He had Justice pinned down in a coulee. He had the long-range weapon, the position. He could take all day if he had to. What was Justice going to do, scale the bluff? Sheer and sandy. Shirke would pick him off that like your grandmother picks daisies.

The bullet hit flesh. It came in sizzling through the willows and it tagged hard. Searing pain bored its way into Ruff's shoulder. He was slammed to the ground, to lie there facedown, breathing in very slowly, very carefully.

Dead? He shook his head. No, not dead. The dead don't feel pain like that. Horrible, red-hot pain. How bad, then? he wondered silently.

It felt very bad, very bad indeed, but then they all do. A gunshot wound is never pleasant. He tried to turn his head, to look at it and see what had happened out there where pain had its birth. It wasn't so easy turning his head.

He could feel the blood seeping slowly out of that shoulder. Blood that ran through a hole in his buckskin shirt into the white-gray sand beneath him. Ruff stared at the wound. When he breathed, the sand moved before his nostrils. The shoulder was on fire.

Damn Hadji.

Ruff shook his head, lifting it from the sand. He could feel a crust of sand on the right side of his face. He didn't pay any attention to it, no more than he paid to the dragonfly humming past or the slowly moving black beetle near his left hand. The pain made all of that immaterial.

He sat up, hair hanging in his eyes, and taking the skinning knife, he savagely ripped open the shoulder of his shirt to see the raw thing that was his arm.

The bullet had come in cleanly from behind, but it had torn up some meat coming out. It hurt like hell and it was bleeding. Ruff wondered if there was a chance he was going to lose it, which was funny, considering how close he was to losing it all.

There wasn't a lot to do about the wound. He tied it with his scarf, using his good arm and his teeth. A child could have done better. It did nothing to stop the hurting.

His head came around sharply. He sat listening, watching. There was a horse in the brush out there.

A horse, and that meant Shirke. Ruff tried to rise, made it on the second attempt, and started moving, moving anywhere so long as it wasn't where he went down. Shirke would have marked that spot well.

He was circling, moving through the brush, stumbling as he went. The sky was nearly blue now, though the coulee was in deep shadow.

Ruff staggered, went down, and fought his way to his feet again to continue on, the Colt held loosely in his right hand.

The horse—he could still hear the horse, which made no sense unless he had walked in a complete circle.

Or unless it was Hadji!

And it was. He saw the sleek black hide through the willows, which were silver in the morning light. He started that way, head thrown back, holding his shoulder as he moved. Once he was mounted . . .

The man on Hadji's back was Connolly, Shirke's right hand. His eye gleamed as he lifted his rifle to fire. As he brought the Winchester up, Hadji reached back and bit the outlaw's leg—hard. The outlaw yelled and his gun discharged, but the bullet went far wide. Ruff, firing from one knee, blew Connolly from the horse; he hit the sand, to bleed his life away in a lonesome coulee in Dakota Territory.

Ruff had his horse. His luck was turning. He somehow got up onto the black, his body screaming out with pain as he swung up. Then he slapped heels to Hadji, and the big gelding leapt into motion, breaking through the brush blindly as Ruff clung to its mane.

A bullet from in front of Ruff cut brush around him; he ducked low, turning Hadji toward the near bluff. It was steep, very steep ahead of him.

"Come on, you bastard," Ruff whispered to the horse, "if you've ever done anything right in your miserable life."

Hadji's eyes were wide. Ruff guided it toward the uneven sandy bluff. There seemed no way up, but Justice was committed now—there was no way back.

Shirke was down there, and any other people he might have left. Justice didn't have much fight in him—he had to get the hell out of that canyon.

The black started up the bluff, slid back, continued as Ruff heeled it angrily, sliding and sinking to its knees, fighting free. Sand sprayed into the air and rifle fire peppered the bluff around Justice. It seemed impossible, far too steep, but the big horse had the will and he had the strength.

Suddenly he was up and over and onto the flat plains, running as only Hadji could run. Until he stepped into the prairie-dog hole and the horrible snapping sound reached Ruff's ears just before he was pitched through the air to land flat on his back, his gun lost somewhere. His shoulder flashed terrible signals to his brain, which reeled and spun and filled with thousands of yellow whirling dots.

Ruff Justice found his way to his feet, but it wasn't going to help any. Hadji was down with a broken leg and his pistol was gone.

And from out of the haze of morning Dallas Shirke was closing down on Ruff, who could only stand there, blood trickling from his shoulder, watching.

He braced himself and looked to the far skies, to the mountains he wouldn't climb again. Then briefly he closed his eyes, saying a few good-byes.

The rifle cracked and the report echoed across the prairie endlessly. Dust sifted through the air. A meadowlark called distantly.

Ruff Justice opened his eyes to see Dallas Shirke dead on the ground fifty feet from where he stood, and riding toward him across the grass the warrior, the Crow, the old man.

Washta!

Washta had his Winchester across his saddlebows. His paint pony looked lathered. Washta's eyes were sharp, the lines around them deep.

"Got him, did you?" Ruff asked. Why was the world tilting underfoot? His voice came from out of a deep tunnel.

"How bad you hit, Ruffin Justice?" Washta asked.

"Pretty damn bad."

The Crow swung down. "Better let me see to it. I don't want you to fulfill my prophecy. Not on this morning. Fine bright morning."

"The horse, Washta. Take care of the black first, will you?"

Washta looked to Hadji. "Sure," he said, and he walked to him, putting the muzzle of the Winchester inside the black's ear. The report sounded dirty. Ruff felt his stomach turn over.

"He wasn't such a bad horse," Justice said. Then he didn't say anything else for a while. Someone came and put the black bag over his head and sent him spinning through the feather-filled tunnel on the other side of the moon.

He didn't fight it at all. There's no pain way back there.

17

IT WAS A LONG, long way back to Tom Valdez's trading post. Washta rigged up a travois behind his little paint pony and Ruff rode back there, jouncing along, passing through alternate periods of extreme pain and discomfort and black unconsciousness. He recalled feeling hot, so hot that he thought there was a brushfire burning somewhere, recalled Washta holding his head up, giving him water, recalled his voice.

"Do not fulfill my prophecy, tall man. Do not walk the Hanging Road just yet."

There was a night and then there was a day, confused in time, the pale moon hanging beneath the sun in a bright sky above a dark land. Alongside the trail thousands of dark-eyed women wrapped in blankets watched as Washta rode his pony southward, dragging its burden behind. Ruff knew the names of everyone, but he didn't dare speak any of them.

It was bad luck, and when you had bad luck, you died.

There was another night and another day, and then a hundred years on, they pulled into Tom Valdez's trading post and a lot of people came out clucking and bustling around, stirring up the dust.

Carla Valdez was there and she looked strained, very strained. Ruff tried to ask her why that was, but she was busy ripping open his shirt with a pair of scissors, shouting something.

"It's all right," Justice said, and he touched Carla's handsome mahogany face. She smiled and the sun set, the world going dark.

When he came around next, he was lying in a bed in Tom Valdez's place, upstairs, the window open so that he could see past the log walls toward the prairie. Ruff didn't know why anyone would want to look at prairie. He didn't know why anyone would fight Indians or outlaws or ride with the cavalry into war or ride through bad weather across endless open earth beneath a hot, mocking sun. He didn't know why anyone would want to be Ruff Justice.

When the door opened, a woman came in, a woman who looked very much like Wendy Warren, except this woman was combed and brushed, her face scrubbed, her hair washed and pinned up, her clothes neat and attractive—a yellow skirt and frilly white blouse. She smelled like violets and she came to his bedside carrying a tray.

"Hi, Wendy."

"Hi yourself." There were sudden tears in her eyes and she bent low to take his hand, kiss it, and wet it with her lips and her tears.

"What's up?" Was that his voice, that dry croak?

"Why, damn you, you almost died, Ruffin T. Justice."

"That makes you mad? Or the fact that I didn't?"

"No jokes." She turned her back. "Damn it all, no jokes."

"All right. No jokes."

"Want some coffee?"

"You'd better believe it." He tried to sit up but didn't make it. There didn't seem to be any blood in his body. Wendy helped him, propping him up with

170

a second pillow. Then she poured some chickory coffee in a white ceramic mug. There were some tamales and frijoles with lots of melted cheese on the tray as well, and Ruff eyed the food greedily.

"Is that for me?" he asked.

"If you think you can handle it."

"Give me a chance," he answered, but something happened then and he closed his eyes, balancing the cup of coffee on his chest. He had his eyes closed for only a second, but when he opened them again, it was dark. Someone had closed the windows.

"Where're my tamales?" he asked in that croaky voice, and the shadow of a woman got up from her bedside chair to pass in front of the dimly glowing lantern and go out. She was back again in fifteen minutes.

Wendy turned up the lamp and gave him the tray and he ate. He ate until he thought he would burst, and then, warm, full, healing, he went to sleep again.

They told him it was five days altogether before he was feeling spunky enough to try getting up from that bed. It might have been a hundred. He felt as if he had never used his body before. He swung his feet to the floor and sat there, head reeling. That was how Wendy found him.

"I leave for ten minutes and this is what you do?" she scolded.

"It was a mistake," he said, "definitely a mistake."

"Well, then, lie down, crazy man." She came to him to help him do that.

"No. I made it this far."

"You won't make it any farther."

"Give me a hand. I can't abide staying in bed any longer, Wendy."

"You'll fall."

"At least I'll be out of bed."

"You're crazy, you know that," she said again. But there was no point in arguing with him. He was going to get up and that was that. She hooked his good arm and let him brace himself against her. Then he rose, stood there woozily, and took three steps.

"You see," he told her. "Nothing to it."

"Fine. Now where are you going?"

"Back to bed."

The next morning he was able to make it down to the breakfast table in his nightshirt and trousers and eat with Jeff Warren and Wendy, Grover Suggs and Tom Valdez. He couldn't stay up long—by noon he was back in bed—but on the following day he rose alone, shaved one-handed, dressed, and came down looking every bit his old self except for the pallor and the awkward way he held his arm.

"Doc—so he calls himself—wanted to saw it off," Tom told Justice. "I figured you'd rather cash in than go on with one wing, a man in your line of work. I told him so. Myself, I could live with a lost limb—so what? But you weren't awake to tell us what to do, so I had to make a decision. That was it. I guess it's what put you into the bad fever, though."

"Thanks, Tom."

"Don't thank me. Thank Carla, she did more for you than you'll ever know. Her and that Warren woman—I had the wrong idea about her, Ruff, you know that? Or else she's changed a hell of a lot."

"Some of each, I expect."

After breakfast Ruff sat out on the porch with the man who saved his life, the old Crow Indian, Washta. Washta had a cob pipe he filled from time to time. Every once in a while he would reach for a small jug he had beside his chair.

"I feel ten years younger. Great fun," Washta said, puffing at his pipe.

"Great fun, huh?"

"Well, it was, Ruffin, wasn't it? As long as you came back alive. I came back alive."

"When do we go again?" Ruffin asked.

Washta laughed. "No more! Now I sit and wait for winter. That was my last ride, my last hunt, and a good one to tell tales of."

Jeff Warren came out and he stood looking to the hills. It was sunny, dry, cool. A dust devil moved across Tom's yard, swirling and dancing. Finally the kid spoke.

"I guess you think I'm an ass, Mister Justice."

"No, Jeff, I don't."

"I know better—the way I was carrying on." He smiled despondently.

"Listen, Jeff, I've seen a hell of a lot of men act worse. You get into a situation new to you, your nerves are acting up and you have to put on a front. Maybe you felt I was challenging you, I don't know, I'm sure you didn't trust me completely, but why should you?"

Jeff tried to interrupt and Justice held up a hand. "Let me go on. You didn't know me from Adam and you were trying to protect your interests. I don't think you were an ass, no. The mistakes you made were from being green. Nobody can help that."

"You mean you aren't holding a grudge?" the kid asked in disbelief.

"What's that get me? No, I'm not holding a grudge—and don't trust the next stranger you run into either." Then Ruff stuck out his hand and Jeff Warren took it in amazement.

After the kid was gone, Washta said, "You tell good stories, Justice."

"Oh, how so?"

"The kid." Washta nodded. "He was a big pain in the ass."

Ruff grinned and nodded. Then he closed his eyes and dozed in the warm sunlight until evening.

In the morning the cavalry patrol came into Donovan's. They were out of Fort Rice, not Fort Lincoln, so Justice didn't know them all. But he knew their officer, Lt. Carson Seales. He was young, tough, determined, and ambitious. He wasn't much of a post soldier, but he was good in the field, very good. He was also supposed to be a little bloodthirsty.

They streamed in, forty soldiers, dusty and dirty. There were wounded with them, the reason they had stopped at Tom Valdez's place.

Lt. Seales swung down and walked to the porch, where he saluted Tom with his gloves.

"We need lodging for half a dozen wounded men, Valdez. And we would like to have some supplies."

"Very well, come on in."

"See some action?" Ruff asked.

Seales looked the scout up and down, trying to place the tall man. Finally he did. "Justice?" Ruff nodded. "Yes, we saw some action. Tell MacEnroe we're covering his tail."

"I'll tell *Colonel* MacEnroe that Lieutenant Seales is covering his tail," Ruff said dryly. Seales' eyes narrowed a little.

"Where was the fighting?" Jeff Warren asked.

"Frenchman's Pass," Seales said offhandedly. Ruff felt something go cold and hard inside him. "Cheyenne renegades under Blood Lance."

"How'd you find them way out there?"

"A month or so back a man named Shirke wrote a letter to the camp commander. He said he had it on good authority that White Badger and Blood Lance were holed up there. He proved to be right. If I meet up with this Shirke, I'd like to shake his hand."

"I wish you would meet up with him," Wendy Warren said. Seales didn't get that. He spent a few minutes eyeing Wendy very carefully instead.

"Did you get him?" Ruff asked when it appeared no one else would.

"Blood Lance? Yeah, we got him. Him and his brother both." Seales was puffed up with his triumph.

Ruff turned away before he could say anything else. After all, Seales had done his job. Ruff might have done the same thing. He stood silently, though, thinking of a tin box up along Frenchman's. A tin box with a rotted piece of parchment in it.

The injured cavalry soldiers were being helped through the door and it sort of broke up the conversation. Suggs, the Warrens, Justice, and Tom Valdez sat around just looking at one another. When Justice couldn't take any more of that, he got up and went out the back door to dump a bucket of well water over his head to try to cool things off.

He didn't see Lt. Seales again until the patrol was ready to leave. "You're welcome to ride with us, be a little safer," Seales said, "especially with a lady along." He managed to make that sound dirty.

"No," Ruff answered. "Thanks, but we'll go back on our own."

"You could check with the others, see what they want." Seales tugged his dashingly shaped hat on.

"I will, but I think I know what their answer will be. Thanks, thanks anyway." Then Ruff turned on his heel and walked away, leaving Seales to wonder what caused the sour expression on the scout's face. He rode out half an hour later without discovering the reason.

"You could have told him," Wendy said.

"It wouldn't have made any difference. Not to him."

"What do we do now?" she asked after a minute. They stood outside, watching the army patrol vanish against the pale horizon, watching the settling dust.

"Go home," was what Ruff Justice told her.

It was time. Another person overheard that short conversation. She stood in the shadows, hands folded, a small person with dark eyes. She had been very patient as Ruff healed, but at five you have only so much patience. Now Marie came forward shyly, eagerly. She tugged at his sleeve and with a tiny finger called him aside.

Ruff crouched down and looked into those dark, too-serious eyes.

"What is it, Marie?"

"Please, Mister Justice, are we going home? To see Grandfather?"

"Yes, yes, we are. And right now. You just tell Carla to give you a few pieces of molasses candy for the trail, get your doll and that new dress. We'll be leaving before you can say Jack Robinson."

"Today?"

"Yes, today."

"Right now?"

"Right now."

"Really?"

"Really. Now you quit gabbin' and get going, or you'll be standing here talking when we're gone."

He picked her up, kissed her nose, and set her down again. With a little squeal of sheer pleasure she went running off. Ruff watched her thoughtfully, wondering if she would even know her grandfather, the stove-up old man he had become. He shook his head and walked back to Wendy.

"Do I pack up too?" she asked.

"You do."

"And do I get molasses candy?"

"All you can eat. And then some."

"And do I get a kiss on my nose?"

She got one, but it wasn't on the nose and it lasted just a little longer than Marie's had. When they left, there was a paper bag in Ruff's hand and he gave it to her just to prove he didn't play favorites. She peeked in.

"Molasses candy?"

"Molasses candy."

It took them two days more to travel south to where it had begun. Justice left the Warren party at the Bismarck Hotel, hearing Wendy order fifty gallons of *boiling*-hot water for a bath as he went out the door with Marie tightly holding his hand.

Ruff got wearily back into the saddle of the little dun pony he had gotten from Tom Valdez, pulled Marie up behind him, and headed toward Fort Lincoln.

"Will Grandfather be waiting for us?" Marie asked.

Ruff looked back at the girl, the girl who had endured so much and had more to suffer yet.

"Yes. They said he was staying out at Lincoln."

"I hope he'll be happy," she said, sounding slightly worried. "Happy to see me."

"Honey, if you knew what he's done to try to find you . . . Of course he'll be happy."

"I might be . . . What if I'm all different than before?"

Ruff Justice told her. "It won't matter. Not a bit. He's your grandpa, and it just won't matter. Would it matter to you," Ruff tried, "if *he* had changed? Changed a lot?"

She gave that long, serious consideration. "No,"

she said at last. "He's my grandpa. It wouldn't matter at all."

Ruff smiled, but the smile faded as he turned his head away. They didn't speak again all the way to Fort Lincoln. He wouldn't have even known she was there except for the slight pressure of her arms holding on to him.

Someone must have seen him coming from a distance because, as they rode through the main gate of Fort Lincoln, Ruff Justice could see Sgt. Pierce and Col. MacEnroe standing on the plankwalk before the colonel's office, shading their eyes, and beside them a hopeful, anxious, joyful old man with a patch over one eye and a cane between his two gnarled hands. Ruff felt the pressure of Marie's arms increase.

She whispered, "Is that him? Is *that* my grandfather?"

"Yes." Ruff slowed the little dun horse. "Has he changed too much?"

"He is," she said with determination, "my grandpa."

Ruff rode that dun right up to the plankwalk and swung the girl down with one hand. She started up the steps, hesitated, and then rushed into the old man's arms. He held her for a long while, and when he looked up, there were tears in his eyes, unashamed tears.

Ruff Justice swung down, nodded once to Martin Spence, and tramped into the orderly room, past Col. MacEnroe and into the inner office, where he sat silently, alone, for a long while. Finally MacEnroe showed up, poured himself a drink, and sat down.

"Well?" the colonel said at last.

"I want some time off."

"All right. Are you hurt?"

"Took a bullet. It's healing."

The colonel took another drink. "That was big,

178

Ruff. Very big. Why don't you go out and look at them?"

"No. It's over. It's their life now, not mine."

"Hard, aren't you?"

"Yes, real hard," Ruff answered.

The colonel on occasion took three drinks together. On this occasion he did, pouring the last, putting the bottle away.

"What's the trouble, Ruffin?"

"Blood Lance. He was killed, you know."

"No, I didn't."

"He was." Ruff told the colonel the whole story. The officer sat virtually unmoving, his chin on his folded knuckles, listening. The colonel was a practical man. When Justice was through, he said, "I'm going to write a letter, Ruff. A lot of letters. I'm going to get that treaty written up again and brought out here. I'm going to see that what remains of Blood Lance's band of Cheyenne receives what is due them. Their women and children, if the warriors can't any longer."

If the colonel said it, he meant it. Ruff nodded. It wasn't a lot of compensation, but it was the best anyone could do.

"He said that, did he?" the colonel asked in a different tone.

"Who?"

"Lieutenant Seales. He said he covered my tail, did he?"

"That is what he said."

"Why, damn it all! That's another letter I'm going to write. No. I'm going to pay a visit to Fort Rice." Then the prime idea occurred to him. "No, by thunder! I'm going to have Lieutenant Carson Seales transferred to Fort Lincoln!" He chuckled softly, evilly, then bellowed at the closed office door,

"Sergeant Pierce, bring me some request forms. We're short an officer, and by God I mean to have one!"

Ruff rose and left. The colonel didn't seem to notice. He was still chuckling with devious delight. Outside, it was clear and cold, the shadows growing longer.

Across the parade ground Ruff Justice saw an old man and a very young girl walking side by side, holding hands. Ruff unhitched the dun and swung aboard, turning the little horse toward Bismarck. Maybe Wendy was through with her bath by now. If not, maybe she could use some help.

The town was beginning to quiet down by the time Ruff reached it. Most of the stores were closed up, the ranchers and folks from the outlying communities having started home. It was still early for the saloon trade. There was only a single horse, a buckboard with a very competent, middle-aged female driver, a kid or two scurrying home with a schoolbook, one red dog.

Ruff looked to the upstairs rooms of the Bismarck Hotel and smiled. Maybe a bath would do *him* good. Was there room for two in those zinc tubs?

He swung down and loosely tied the dun, stepped up onto the boardwalk, and came face to face with Tiny Larch.

"Hello, Justice. Remember me?"

"I remember you. Your breath isn't any better than last time."

"Still the smart ass."

"Leave it alone, Larch, it isn't worth it."

"It is to me."

"No it's not. Not to anybody."

"You going to hurt me again?" Larch demanded.

"Likely not, with the shape I'm in, but why find out? Wander on down the street, I'll stand for drinks."

"Going to whip both of us?" Tiny Larch asked even more loudly, and Ruff felt cold fingers crawl up his spine. Turning a quarter away from Tiny, he saw big Dan Larch coming toward them. And in his hand was a club.

"We going to beat you to death, Justice," Tiny Larch said, and then he swung. He swung and his meaty fist caught Ruff Justice flush on the wounded shoulder. Justice screamed with pain and toppled backward down the wooden steps to lie in Bismarck's Main Street watching the savage face of Tiny Larch light up with brutal glee.

"I'll finish him, Tiny," Dan Larch said, and he shoved his brother aside. Dan Larch, vast and bearlike, lifted the club he held and Ruff Justice drew. He drew his Colt and drilled a .44-caliber hole in Dan Larch's forehead. The big man gurgled something and staggered backward to slump against the steps and die.

With a roar Tiny Larch drew his own gun and fired at Ruff, the bullet kicking up dirt beside Justice's head. Ruff switched his muzzle to Tiny and fired. Three times he fired as Tiny Larch came toward him, his mouth spilling blood. Tiny lifted his gun, staggered back, and started forward again. When the third bullet stopped his heart, he fell backward to lie beside his brother, bleeding crimson against the weathered gray steps of the Bismarck Hotel.

People were coming on the run now, the marshal and several uniformed soldiers. They picked Ruff up and, in doing so, jarred his shoulder again.

Then Wendy was there, hastily dressed, and she clung to him for a long minute.

"Oh, Ruff! I thought they had you that time. Your shoulder! You need to see a doctor."

"I need to see you," he said quietly. He turned her

and started with her toward the hotel, past the dead men and the gawking crowd. "I need you, Wendy. Now."

"Ruff! In your condition? Are you sure you can?"

"Woman," Ruff Justice said, "I am known far and wide as a man with the natural ability to rise to any occasion."

And he proved it.

WESTWARD HO!

The following is the opening section from the
next novel in the gun-blazing, action-packed new
Ruff Justice series from Signet:

RUFF JUSTICE #20: THE SONORA BADMAN

Fort Bowie, Arizona Territory

The sun went down with a flourish and the dogs
of the tiny Spanish town yapped in appreciation.
The long-legged woman with the bright, sensuous
smile came out of the adobe house and turned for
Ruff Justice, who took it all in. She wore a striped
skirt and a white blouse that came down off the
shoulders, revealing smooth coffee-colored skin. Her
hips were full, rounded, and competent. Her breasts
jutted against the fabric of her blouse, lifting it,
making it something more than a few bits of cloth
sewn together, bringing it to a life of its own.

Her name was Alicia.

"Do you like it? My new blouse, Ruffin Justice?"

"I do like it," Ruffin Tecumseh Justice allowed.
"All of it."

They were standing before the adobe house in the dusty yard as the sundown glow reddened the walls of the tilted buildings up and down the crooked street. Beyond the adobes stood Fort Bowie, dismal, sunbaked, trying to maintain its military dignity, not quite managing it.

"You are ready?" she asked. She stepped into his arms and kissed him, her lips light and searching.

"Always ready," he replied.

"No, naughty man." She put her finger on his lips. "Ready to eat?"

"Yes."

Alicia cocked her head to one side and looked again at the tall man before her. He was supposed to be very strong, very *fuerte*, but with her he was always gentle. He was a scout for the army and had been helping them look for Sandfire, an Apache. Yet now he wore a ruffled shirt, dark trousers and coat, a black hat with a huge brim, a string tie. His hair was long and dark, as smooth and pretty as Alicia's own blue-black hair. He wore a mustache that drooped past his jawline. He was tall, very tall and very amusing—yet at times he was far away from Alicia, even when they made love, which he did with great enthusiasm and skill.

Now she hooked his arm with her own, and together, her head on his shoulder, they strode up the dusty street toward the cantina. There Alicia's sister, Rosita, sang; there Uncle Fernando served his famous tamales, made from the succulent flesh of kid roasted over coals in an open pit. That, and much salsa, many tortillas and beans. There she and this Ruff Justice danced around the floor to the mariachi band, to the delight of the onlookers. There they laughed together and then went back to Alicia's house, to her bed, to strip off their clothes and join their heated bodies.

It was hot in the street still. It was late spring in Arizona and it was always hot.

"You are going back soon, back north?" Alicia asked.

"You know I am."

"You must?"

"Yes," Ruff Justice answered.

"But you never found this butcher, Sandfire."

"No, and I don't think we ever would find him. When the Hopi scouts gave it up, I knew I was overmatched. He's lost us and likely's in Mexico now, laughing himself silly over the incompetence of the U.S. cavalry and its civilian scout . . . what was his name?"

He looked at Alicia and frowned, and she laughed, and since it was a lovely laugh and since the night was young and they were going to dance and eat and laugh and make love, Ruff Justice stopped in the middle of the street and kissed her.

"*Ai*, hombre, you take my appetite away."

"Fine. Let's turn around, then."

"No. I told Rosita tonight we would be there. She has a new song."

"All right."

"You are not angry?"

"Of course not. Don't pout either. We'll have a time of it tonight."

"And later . . ."

"Of course." He kissed the top of her head and walked her toward the cantina, which was called La Paloma. Twilight was making purple shadows in the alleyways, beneath the awnings of the buildings. A last effort of the dying sun stretched gold lace across the western horizon, where low clouds hung sheer and dry-looking. Everything looked dry in and around Fort Bowie. Everything was. Water was a precious commodity. It wasn't wasted on flowers and shrubs, on livestock. Some of the people didn't believe in wasting it on washing.

Nothing grew out in the wasteland beyond the town. Between Bowie and the Peloncillo Mountains to the east there was only rocky desert stroked here and there with the dull green of yucca or the gray of smoke trees. There was thorny mesquite in abundance, much cholla cactus, some ocotillo, but only the wild things could find sustenance out there.

It was a land Ruff Justice had spent some time in, but he had never grown to like it despite the sometimes spectacular beauty of it.

He was a northern man, a man of the plains, but the army had wanted him down south to help look for the Chiricahua Sandfire, and so he had come.

"You are silent," Alicia said. It was no new mood for this tall man, but it puzzled her and left her feeling alone when he drifted away like that. The young vaqueros of the town never let their attention drift away from Alicia.

"I was thinking of Sandfire again."

"Wishing you had caught him."

"Yes. He's the sort you can't feel pity for. I wish they'd caught him and hung him."

"I wish worse for him," Alicia said with some passion. She had lost two cousins to Sandfire's knife. She shook the anger aside. She had promised that she would not worry about anything tonight.

The cantina was brightly lit. Guitar music drifted out into the street. Several army horses were tied up in front, and inside, all was gaiety. No one else was worried about the failure of the army to capture the cutthroat Chiricahua. The soldiers were happy to be back off the desert, to be drinking green beer and raw tequila, to be eating mountains of hot Mexican food and dancing with the señoritas.

Ruff's own mood lifted as soon as he walked in the door. Sgt. Ward, who had been bitten by a sidewinder on the trek, was there looking pale but cheerful, his right hand still swollen. He waved to Ruff.

Alicia's Uncle Fernando came rushing to greet them, a jovial, bearded man with a potbelly and a single gold tooth.

"Almost late! Hello, Ruffin Justice. Your table was hard to hold tonight, Alicia. Shame. What have you been doing? Never mind, don't tell me, I don't want to know." He was leading them across the crowded room now. Heads lifted and men made cracks to Ruff, who smiled back or waved. "Your sister is going on in five minutes. How will you eat now? You'll have to wait until after."

They had arrived at a corner table, small, round, empty. Uncle Fernando continued to chatter on as he held out Alicia's chair for her, shouted something in Spanish to a bartender, and then bustled away.

Alicia laughed. "Such a busy man. He didn't ask what I wanted to drink. Well, he'll remember after a while and bring my favorite wine."

The band struck up a new song and there was time for one more dance before Rosita went on. Ruff rose and started to help Alicia up.

It was then the trouble started across the room.

The cantina door opened and closed as it had been doing constantly, but there was something about the way it happened, the authoritative sound as it slapped closed perhaps, that caused people to stop what they were doing and glance that way, knowing that something violent was about to intrude on their world of merriment.

Ruff felt it too. But when he looked to the door, he saw only two enlisted men and their officer. All held drawn guns, however, and the officer, a tight-lipped, narrow-eyed lieutenant, wore an armband that read "OD," officer of the day.

Their eyes were fixed on a man across the cantina, a man with wide shoulders, square red-bearded face, receding hair, and a plump Mexican woman on his lap. Behind him the window reflected the man's back and shoulders, and Justice imagined he saw the muscles tense beneath the big man's blue uniform.

The officer walked right up to the table, his men behind him.

"Corporal McCoy, I am placing you under arrest."

"You're what?" The corporal laughed in a way that revealed his lack of fear. There wasn't anything to indicate apprehension in McCoy's manner. He still hugged the señorita, who had stopped giggling and seemed badly to want to leave. McCoy held her to him.

"You heard me well enough. I'm placing you under arrest. Please rise and surrender your sidearm."

Then Dutch McCoy threw back his head and laughed again, but before he had stopped laughing, he moved. He drew his army-issue Schofield revolver and fired point-blank into the lieutenant's face.

The officer wore a mask of blood as he turned briefly toward Justice, arms outstretched as if pleading for help, and dropped to the floor, dead.

McCoy meanwhile had thrown the Mexican woman at the two enlisted men, one of whom fired wildly into the ceiling as McCoy, arm over his face, leapt through the window behind him in a shower of glass.

There was a moment's awed silence, mass immobility, then the soldiers raced for the window, surged toward the door. But it was already dark outside and Dutch McCoy was gone into the desert, leaving his kill behind.

And Ruff Justice had the sudden feeling that he wouldn't be going home as soon as he had thought.

He was right about that. The next day Maj. John Cavendish, Bowie's thoughtful-appearing, small commander, called the scout into his office. It was under ninety inside the headquarters building for a change, but then it was scarcely ten o'clock in the morning. Ruff, wearing buckskin trousers and a white cotton shirt, a belt gun—a long-barreled Colt .44 revolver—a bowie knife, and a tan-colored hat, carrying a sheathed .56 Spencer repeating rifle, entered the office without knocking.

"I want him," Cavendish said.

"You sent out a patrol?"

"He beat them to the border. By now he's in Sonora," the major replied. "I had a good young officer, a Lieutenant Oberlies, in charge of that patrol. He exceeded standing orders and went fifteen miles—at a minimum—into Mexico. He's been reprimanded for that. Had it been me, I would have kept going anyway and the hell with it. I also would have lost some rank. We can't rely on the Mexican authorities to do much. We need a civilian. You."

"I was supposed to head back toward Dakota."

"I'll take care of that. What's the matter, Justice, lost your taste for the desert?"

Ruff smiled. "You could say that."

"Well, I don't blame you a bit." Cavendish spoke quickly, clipping off his words. He toyed with a cigar he never lit. "But I want McCoy. He killed one of my officers. I want him badly."

"What made him do it? What was he supposed to be arrested for?" Justice wanted to know. "It was a violent reaction if it was only a minor infraction."

"McCoy has another name. VanPelt. Under that name he's wanted for murder, arson, and bank robbery in Texas. He enlisted to escape from the law. Many do, you know."

"Yes, sir. So I've heard."

"Well, he was spotted by someone who knew him. A new trooper. He reported McCoy to me yesterday. Since that time another matter has come to light. On questioning McCoy's cronies I discovered that he had plans to hold up the army payroll on the fifth of the month. McCoy and four other troopers. He knew he'd hang if he was arrested. That's what caused him to go to gunplay."

"And now he's gone."

"Temporarily."

"Sir?" Ruff asked, though he knew what the man meant.

"You're going to drop down to Sonora and pick him up for us, aren't you?" Cavendish said mildly. And that was the way he gave his commands.

The northern plains would have to wait for a bit. So would Alicia. Ruff Justice rose and nodded a good-bye. Then he went out onto the plankwalk in front of Fort Bowie's orderly room and stood looking southward, toward Mexico, toward Sonora.

Exciting Westerns by Jon Sharpe

JOIN THE *RUFF JUSTICE* READERS' PANEL

Help us bring you more of the books you like by filling out this survey and mailing it in today.

1. Book Title: _____

   Book #: _____

2. Using the scale below, how would you rate this book on the following features? Please write in one rating from 0-10 for each feature in the spaces provided.

POOR		NOT SO GOOD			O.K.			GOOD		EXCEL-LENT
0	1	2	3	4	5	6	7	8	9	10

RATING

Overall opinion of book .... _____
Plot/Story .... _____
Setting/Location .... _____
Writing Style .... _____
Character Development .... _____
Conclusion/Ending .... _____
Scene on Front Cover .... _____

3. About how many western books do you buy for yourself each month? _____

4. How would you classify yourself as a reader of westerns? I am a ( ) light ( ) medium ( ) heavy reader.

5. What is your education?
   ( ) High School (or less)   ( ) 4 yrs. college
   ( ) 2 yrs. college   ( ) Post Graduate

6. Age _____   7. Sex: ( ) Male ( ) Female

Please Print Name_____

Address_____

City _____ State _____ Zip _____

Phone # ( )_____

Thank you. Please send to New American Library, Research Dept., 1633 Broadway, New York, NY 10019.